normal in their lives, and, while, they have all been kind of beaten up in different ways, each carries inside the flame of hope and beauty. They bravely try for that place where normal is not so important. Literally and figuratively they find a home and a family of friends where they can sing out loud.

It's about place; meaning; friends; acceptance; and the family you make for yourself as you go through life. I liked it basically because I liked the characters and the idea of finding a haven where normal is not required.

SANDI SOX, poet

I read this book from cover to cover on a plane ride back to the States from London. No, I HADN'T gone to Cork in my travels, but I surely wished I had by the end of the novel/my plane ride. Or had I? The characters and places were so clearly drawn that within the first few pages I felt immersed in this other world. And while I appreciated this journey into another culture, it was at least as much about the chemistry and interrelatedness of some people who happened upon each other in this new place. I have no doubt the atmospherics of that part of Ireland are ably represented here, but it is the individuals, and their wishes, longings, dreams and disappointments, that stand strong, making this a very universal story. It is both timely and timeless— exploring, among other themes, the notion of finding the place (within yourself and with others) where you are accepted and admired just for who you are, not merely what you do. The author writes beautifully, simply, evocatively and also complexly—its a total pleasure to go with the story and see where it takes you.

TERRI GLENN, poet

There is an oceanic feel to Mr. Coulson's book. It intentionally blurs the hard, demanding, material world and forces us down (together) to those deep, emotional pools we've all slipped into from time to time. It's a serious look into that world, with its possibilities and dangers. His characters are rich and playful, like river stones shifting and marvelously changing hue just under the surface. Their serendipitous meetings and developing relationships give the story just enough buoyancy in troubled waters (and the same bonds affect the reader, too). This book steps outside the conventional novel and creates it's own, significant tributary.

JOHN MITCHELL, poet

What else could you ask for in a summer read? Escape, fresh start, and pleasures for the soul (and the body) ... Expect a twisty trip with lively characters.

KIM TOWNSEL, writer

Elegantly written; weaving together Magic Realism and crazy hopefulness amidst very dark stuff. RED JUMBO hooked me from the elegantly California start. There are tons of literary Easter eggs hidden in this book—I can feel it. I'm thinking nothing is left undone here, it's a web of interconnectedness; it's immediate, of the now, yet also acknowledges the histories of things remembered, and I love the guest appearances. I sailed through this book! It has great flow, and I loved being along on that very communal ride after all this time being in pandemic mode. It's interesting how Coulson wove all the parts together; there's claustrophobia and the weight of personal pasts, and then it opens up into expanding spaces ... the open road ... Kansas ...   Aunt Arctica's endless mansion of inclusion, *so* many symbols and sign posts, even death has no hold on those who supposedly crossed over—even egregious sins can maybe be forgiven. The magical realism is fabulous! It's also crazy hopeful, amidst some very dark stuff. Bravo!

SARA GARDNER-GAIL, artist

In THE MIDWEST HOTEL, poet Chris Coulson has created a variety of personae that teach and delight a reader. From a woman wanting her husband to join her in a dance, to a recovered alcoholic who describes "those years were like living in a cave," he carves characters with wit and powers of observation akin to Mark Twain's. This work will catch your emotions. Be prepared to Chuckle, laugh out loud, or shed a tear.

LINDSEY MARTIN-BOWEN
author of *Inside Virgil's Garage* and
Standing on the Edge of the World

Chris Coulson's words make you angry and sad, laugh out loud happy, and mostly stare at the page in astonishment telling yourself the world he describes, so tantalizingly familiar, simply can't be.

PETER SCHUYLER, writer and filmmaker

For me, Chris Coulson is the American *kirjanik*, which means American Writer in my native Estonian. His witty, gritty writing is in places poetic, in places epic. Who wouldn't fall in love with a Joseph Campbell-inspired, bliss-seeking bear, a suicidal fly, a compassionate Ford Van, and all the other characters talking to us through Chris' poetry? They all make my world instantly bigger and better. After all life's unavoidable, inevitable drama and trauma, who wouldn't love writing that's open, brave, vulnerable, and understanding?

AIRI LOOMAN
linguist, translator, poetry blogger

THE MIDWEST HOTEL is new and funny and wise, all the things a poem should be, and all those things American poetry has become. It's Beat. Coulson plays sky pilot and points his prose toward the house of the rising sun. He writes, "... you wake up and your brain feels like it's between radio stations." The lines are personal. I can't imagine this book surviving the Iowa Writers' Workshop, which is a damn good thing. This guy writes his own stuff: unapproved, non-filtered, and as down hard as Charles Bukowski, and not the movie version.

JEFF SHEAR, author of
The Jackson Guild Saga

Nothing Normal in Cork

Nothing Normal in Cork

a novel by

Chris Coulson

PINEHEAD PRESS

NOTHING NORMAL IN CORK

PINEHEAD PRESS
www.pineheadpress.com

ISBN: 979-8-9880528-0-7 (paperback)
ISBN: 978-0-9894236-9-4 (epub)
Library of Congress Control Number: 2010900944

Cover illustration and design
© 2025 by Chris Coulson

Author photo by Susan Emshwiller

For my Beautiful Soulful Wild
Darling Susan

who danced with me in the Midwest Hotel
(all it took was a cigar and a gas station)

I'll never want another dance partner.

CORK, again. Let me introduce you.

I'm not even remotely Irish. I was in eastern Kansas when Ireland—the music, the sound and rhythm of that way of talking, the sense of humor and life-widening joy (in spite of *whatever)*, the writing, drinking and singing, the seemingly spontaneous kindness of those people—took hold of me.

My last name is a bit British, there's a Coulson street in London, where I lived for three fast months as a baby, but that's neither here nor there (Ireland *or* England).

I was young, in the lively Johnson County Community College, when my eyes, ears, heart, and sense of bravery were at last opening up to the sun, the moon, women, and also to the rebellious faculty of the English Department, who took me (after class, at night) to a magical place called *The Irish Brigade.* That was Paddy's Day, 1978.

Inside *The Irish Brigade*, I was *somewhere else*, far from my midwestern home, and I needed that. I knew it the second I walked in the door to a pub-full of wild, friendly troublemakers taking the shape of singers, dancers (I learned how to waltz and jig), drinkers (I knew how, but my first Guinness, first Harp Beer, first Jameson's, first Black and Tan happened there), story-tellers, also very good *listeners*—where I saw and heard Irish music, Irish poetry and stories—and all those troublemakers would fall silent and listen. So suddenly silent, so moving. So still. You could hear a shot glass drop.

I fell in love there, had my first kiss there, during my first waltz there—the faculty smiling, cheering me on from the bar.

I carried this all inside me, but didn't get to actual Ireland for years, around 2004. On the way, right up to the moment of landing at the Cork Airport, I was talking to myself—*Don't bring your romantic stereotypes with you, these are people, not types, you might feel let down.* But I was worrying too much. Just like the Irish I met in Kansas City, everyone was warm, open, funny, musical, in the moment, and unforgettable.

Back at the ranch in the California desert, I started to write this book, making up these characters so I could be *with* them. Nothing against the desert or the goats and sheep out back, but I missed Ireland. These people I wrote are still in me, and I still must be in *them*, because they've asked for a celebratory reissue of their book: The 15th Anniversary Edition of *Nothing Normal in Cork.*

Anything to get everyone together again.
Anything for the warmth of community, large or small.
Any excuse for a party!
Anything, anyone, anytime, **CHEERS!**

  love, Chris

Come on, let's go ...

"Lookin' for a brand new start ..."

Listen to the Lion
Van Morrison

Nothing Normal
in Cork

THE BEGINNING, THE END

CHESTER STANDS in his blue corduroy robe looking through the rough window of his stone house and sees almost all of the city below. He checks his new watch from the Cork Airport gift shop, it's nine o'clock so far this morning, which means coffee. Later means beer, but first things first, he thinks, at least I'll *start* normal today with coffee.

And then he remembers that he made a decision to end everything normal in his life.

And he's come to this un-normal city to stick with it.

IT'S NOT TOO LATE

CHESTER LEANS on the cold grey stone windowsill and exhales on the window, fogging out the view of the foggy city. He remembers this decision and sees himself smiling as the little window clears again.

He'd said, "Before I turn fifty, or the morning I do, but either way, not a day beyond that birthday—I STOP BEING NORMAL. Enough is enough."

He watches Cork open up below. The little stores are all different colors and seem to open from left to right, up the street and over the hill, pale yellow lights popping on in each window. The shopkeepers open the front doors and leave them open so they can talk to each other.

Chester thinks of what Rob, his first friend in Cork had said about this, "In this town there are so many pubs that they mostly are all lined up next door to each other because there's no way around that...being that there so many of them, you see what I mean?" He thinks about this remark with its intricate structure and thoroughness, and then Rob himself enters the little stone frame of his window, this window that is the new morning movie of his new town.

ROB

ROB ALWAYS WEARS a combination of green and blue wool and corduroy with a big brown cap that falls over the side of his long, thin face. He wears round gold glasses like his hero John Lennon, and boots so old they seem to be shedding leather strips as he walks. Rob waves into each open shop as he walks along, then, looking up the hill to Chester's house, goes into a deep bow and tip of his hat. After Chester waves back, Rob acts out drinking from an invisible mug and points to the nearest pub, the pub where they met last week, on Chester's first day in town. Then he walks into that pub. Chester turns around to find his pants and sweater.

TOMMY

IN THE PUB, it's just Rob and Tommy so far, but Rob is talking and gesturing with his arms like the room is full and a band is playing.

"Oh, Tommy! I need a bit of the hair of the dog. Where IS that wee little hairless dog of mine?"

Tommy the barman, a very big man with a soft smile, smiles again for Rob's frequent joke about the hairless dog and pours the first Beamish of the day. The first for a customer anyway. He's had his own behind the bar in his favorite glass. The glass he'd stolen on a special night.

Tommy had taken the ferry from Wales across the Irish Sea in the middle of the night not long ago, a one-way ticket on the ferry, and he had ordered a pint of stout in a hurry so he could have it on the top deck and toast the receding coastline, and say goodbye to it. There were many refills at the bar that night after which he'd return to the deck to toast the Irish Sea, then the smokestacks of the ship, then the rain falling hard from the dark sky into the lights of the deck.

And he sang the whole way over, alone up on the deck. Tommy likes to sing but not in front of people, though that is his dream. But standing that night on the top deck at the rear of the ferry with the engines roaring below and the sea crashing and the rain falling and his cap pulled low, he sang as loud as he could and felt the most excitement and freedom he'd ever felt. And he laughed at how drunk he was and didn't feel ashamed of that at all, and he thought *it's not too late.* He thought *I am making this trip and every other soul is downstairs in the warm like any reasonable person would be, but I'm up here in the rain and maybe I will sing in front of people someday! I still think I can. I'll be ready for that someday. And this night is the beginning of that for me. Tonight I sing alone on the sea, but someday there'll be an audience.*

Later that night when the little yellow lights of Wexford started rising in the distance, he toasted the lights and emptied the pint glass, laughing and drunk, smiling and crying and very happy. The glass went inside his coat.

And now Tommy fills his glass fresh as Rob talks to the room from the corner table by the window. Tommy nods to Rob when his loud sentences end, but he's back on that ferry as he watches his stout foam settle down and level off creamy. He feels the cold of that night now and puts on his extra large fuzzy brown wool sweater. He turns to the back bar where his "office" is; legal pads, receipts on a spike, cigar boxes full of pens, cigar boxes full of pub paperwork, cigar boxes full of cigars, and his little radio that wires into small speakers all around the bar. He switches the radio on and Shane MacGowan is in the middle of "A Pair of Brown Eyes." Rob hears this and stops his talk in the middle of a sentence and begins singing along with the song, off-key, pounding the table in rhythm, knocking his glass off the table.

Tommy stands behind the bar, his back to the room, his head down, and he sings too. He closes his eyes and sings softly, trying to keep himself in key, trying to hear if he is or not. He takes a drink from his special glass, then takes out a pen and writes something down. He writes

TOMMY BOY, you can do this and one day you will. You take your time and build up to the day you can do it. You are brave inside and little by little, day by day, you can build it up and bring it out for the others to see. You decided this that night on the Irish Sea and it's to happen. Can't <u>not</u> now. Now go on MISTER BRAVE HEARTY SINGER ... put your CHEST out!

He puts this note in a cigar box he has hidden behind bottles, takes a big swallow of stout, and turns around to the pub again. He forces his left arm up in the air with his fingers extended out and sings a little louder. A little louder than a whisper, but singing.

Rob leaps to his feet, knocks over his table, and sings along with Tommy, eyes big through his John Lennon glasses.

"That's it, Tommy, let it go!"

Tommy walks out into the center of the room and Rob stands in front of him, conducting him, pushing him to get louder, pulling the singing out of him, clapping and stomping the floor.

"Go Tommy, go!"

And now Tommy has his other arm up in the air and he is indeed singing a bit louder and gazing off into the romantic distance, towards an audience, which this morning is a dart board across the pub. Tears are rolling down Rob's face but Tommy keeps singing.

"You're getting better all the time Tommy! I heard you back there behind the bar, singing to yourself, very sort of quiet and shy, but GOOD, mind you, and now you're out here, very theatrical, right in the middle of the room! Go on, keep it up, you know, Tommy—you gotta walk before you crawl, right? I mean, well, you know what I mean ..."

Tommy keeps on singing, and his arms are waving around and Rob is dancing in circles around him and talking to himself, dancing as much to his talking to himself as he is to Tommy's singing, and into this singing comes Chester, glasses fogging up in the warmth of the pub.

"Tommy, where's that little hairless dog?" he says.

ESCAPE IN A FLASH OF GREEN

A BUS STOP in Kinsale.

A short, round woman in a red sweater and a little black hat sits and waits for the Cork bus. She fiddles with her bags, checks her watch, and pulls her ticket out of her purse to make sure she has it ready for the driver. She looks down the street and up to the second floor of her old apartment, where she has lived for the last twenty-five years. Even this morning, in her last few moments in the apartment, she pulled the lace curtains back and neatly tied them off at the sill. The next boarder will feel welcomed by this, she thinks. When she arrived here, there were no curtains at all and no furniture, nothing. But Mary will not leave nothing. She has left much more than the curtains and the furniture.

Just these bags, she thinks, *and my lucky black hat is all I'll be taking away*. This makes her smile and feel cocky and free. Cocky and free enough to look across the street into the window of the new Starbucks that has replaced the tea and biscuit room she'd begun and run—for the last twenty-five years.

A low silver car pulls up alongside the bus stop waiting for the light to change. Loud U2 music pulses from inside and vibrates the chrome of the car. The driver, wearing black sunglasses and a black leather jacket and a black beard, drums his fingers on the wheel and glances over at Mary on the bus stop bench. He smiles faintly noticing her tapping her foot with the driving U2 guitars and drums. Then she's sticking out her tongue and he drops the smile.

Mary has made eye contact with the new young manager of the Starbucks who's on a cell phone, and she has her tongue sticking out very pointedly at *him*. The driver turns and looks where Mary is looking. He looks back and forth, then, ignoring the green light, reaches out his big, black-leathered arm and gives Starbucks the finger.

Mary's stare breaks off and she laughs. The driver pumps his fist, then peels out squealing rubber. Mary watches him fly off down the road, admiring the long tire marks he's left behind. Young students in the Starbucks look up from their laptop computers and look at Mary. The young manager is still on the cell phone but not saying a word.

Then the bus comes.

Down the street standing outside Mary's old apartment building, a man watches Mary get on her bus. He watches as she takes one slow step at a time up the steps, as the driver slides her bags into the luggage compartment below. This all takes awhile, but he watches the bus until it crawls up the road, around Kinsale Bay. Then, he goes into her old building and walks up the wooden stairs to her flat.

Inside, he sits on the window seat that looks out over the misty rooftops of Kinsale. He smells perfume in the room. He wonders where she's going. It's dim in the room. She's left a lot behind. Pictures and small framed paintings and her shelf of teacups. There's a single bed with a fuzzy green blanket and pillow, a trunk at the foot of her bed covered with doilies and her collection of ceramic dogs, all lined up and watching the place where she had slept.

He thinks how she was with all the dogs of town and how, often as she walked down the street to her tea room, there would be nine or ten dogs trailing behind her, escorting her to work. She'd go inside, return with nine or ten biscuits from the day before and hand them out. That done, she'd turn on the lights, go to work, and the dogs would break off in different directions and go on to their different lives, still chewing.

The man knows she's never had a dog of her own and she hasn't taken one of her ceramic ones from the room. He picks up one of those dogs and walks around the dark room on the creaking wooden floor, and he looks out the window over the rooftops to where the two-lane road rises from the town and enters the trees towards Cork. He watches as the bus disappears into those trees.

"Where the hell ya goin' Mary?" he says aloud.

Mary watches out the window as the bus flies through the woods making a flash of light green through the glass.

"This man is really flyin' ain't he?" says a friendly white-haired man across the aisle looking out his window. "Really sailin' along!"

He says this for Mary and pulls out a small whiskey bottle from his jacket to toast his observation with her. He takes a long swallow.

Mary looks at her face reflected in the window and she likes what she sees. She didn't know she could still look this excited; not young, *excited.* She thinks her twinkly eyes look like trouble and smiles. She looks over at the man across the aisle to see if he's watching. He isn't, so she jiggles her arms and shoulders with excitement like a little Christmas Eve girl.

The man with the bottle sings with his free hand waving the tune in the air. There are passengers up near the driver quietly riding along, and behind Mary, a young man in black jeans and a black t-shirt and glasses with stiff straight-up orange hair in the back row of the bus, hiding behind a book. Mary looks back at the man with the bottle.

"Might I, ehm, possibly ...?" she nods at his pint bottle of whiskey.

He leans towards her as she asks, then looks where she's nodding.

"Oh Jaysus, why of course, here you go Miss."

He hands it to her openly, not in a bag or hidden in any way. She takes it across the aisle and takes a good swallow, tipping her head way back. Her little black hat falls off and lands on its crown in the aisle. The old white-haired man scrambles quickly down to fetch it, brushing it off and laying it elegantly across his left forearm for Mary.

The young man in the back watches all of this, smiling. He feels as though he hasn't smiled like this in awhile. He smiles that the white hair on the old man sticks straight up in the air, too.

Meanwhile, up front, the bus driver smells the whiskey in the air and winks at himself in the rearview mirror.

And Mary gazes out the window as they fly through the trees.

"Fearless, I am," she whispers. "Fearless."

SMELLING SOMETHING AHEAD

A LITTLE PEPPER-COLORED TERRIER comes running around a long curved street in Cork, runs downhill, and sprints across a bridge over the River Lee. His furry white paws are a blur and he holds his head up, looking around everywhere. When he gets to the other side of the bridge he stops and checks out where he's got to. A squirrel darts across grass and he goes after it. The squirrel disappears into bushes and so the terrier stops and checks everything out again, undiscouraged. He finds a sidewalk and trots along, stopping and sniffing at bus stop benches, shoes and legs there, shopping bags also there, has his head rubbed a bit, and moves on.

He walks and walks, head up, smells something ahead, goes around the corner of a building and down an alley. He tips his head into an open back door of a kitchen, and jumps back at the sound of big metal pots being thrown into a sink. His wondering brown eyes look through the kitchen into the dining room. There's a long wooden table with a chair. The chair is low. On the table is a large package of hamburger.

The pepper dog backs up a step or two, his little white legs trembling a bit. He looks behind him down the alley. He looks down the kitchen into the restaurant again. Then at the package of hamburger. He steps through the door, walks to the low chair, looks around again, and jumps on the chair. With his two front paws on the table, he gets a corner of the hamburger's styrofoam tray in his mouth and drags it to the edge of the table. He pulls it a bit further and has it dangling in his mouth, the meat swinging heavy in his teeth. A burst of laughter comes from the restaurant, a walking thumping on the floor comes closer, and he's gone out the back door with the meat clenched in his teeth, and down the alley.

Finding a low window well, the pepper dog gently drops the package, then himself, down a foot and out of sight from the street and the alley. With a paw he begins to strip away the plastic wrap and lick at the meat. More stripping, more licking, then he bites off a large corner of hamburger and chews happily, the perfect tiny white teeth bared and grinding away, his glassy eyes blissful, looking up along the walls of the alley to the sky.

Soon, and only half the little mountain of hamburger gone, the dog is stretched out, belly up, on some dry leaves in the well, asleep. His furry white chest breathes up and down, slowly, peacefully. His paws run a little in the air, maybe remembering the long curved road and his flying across the bridge, the smells of the river and the city coming into his nose as he runs.

A cool breeze comes down the alley and blows around the little white hairs of the dog's chest and face, and he sneezes in his sleep, and keeps sleeping. Flies have found the meat now too, and are taking their time moving across the hills of food, and then they are kicked off the hills. The flies are what especially angers the cook, and he kicks the side of the window well, waking up the dog.

"GODDAMN fuckin' flies and dogs and fuckin' bums after my goddamn fuckin' MEAT!" He kicks the well again, hard, and the dog is on its feet and in a corner with his feet all together and his head down, shaking all over. "OUT! Fuckin' OUT of there you little bastard, little meat-stealin' bastard of a dog." The cook's big hand comes fast under the dog's chest and grabs his ribs, making the dog cry out. Fast, the cook strides down the alley, dropping the rest of the hamburger in a trash can, and turns back into his kitchen.

The cook grabs open a door and flings the dog to the floor, where he slides into a bunch of mops and brooms and pails and he crouches down low and shaking, his head away from the cook and the kitchen light. The door slams shut, and he's in the dark, shaking, listening, his little brown eyes wondering but not seeing.

The dog sits bunched up and crouching in a corner of the cook's truck bed. He can smell the river again, but he doesn't look above the truck bed walls to the river or the sky. He looks down and keeps his eyes on the rusty metal floor as the cook speeds and jerks through traffic.

At last the truck has stopped and the cook has his rough hands on the dog's little ribs again, squeezing him. He carries him into a low building by the bus station and swings him up onto a tall white counter, and the dog stands there under bright ceiling lights, the little legs shaking and skinny.

"No tags, eatin' my friggin' hamburger meat he was." The cook has his arms folded and he's waiting for a thank you from the shelter for not killing the dog in the alley. It doesn't come.

On the other side of the counter, now softly stroking the dog's head, is a tall red-haired woman with sunglasses on, and she's not taking them off. She's been eating a fat roast beef sandwich with cheese and lettuce leaking out all around the edges of the bread.

"Thanks, Brendan," she says, looking up at the cook, her sunglasses still on. The dog is shaking hard through his legs and hips, and he looks back at the cook, his eyes low and looking up through dainty eyelashes. But he smells the cheese and beef in the shelter director's hand.

"You're a regular sort of Nelson Mandela, you are," she says through the impenetrable dark and sexy glasses, smiling.

Now the cook's hands are on his hips. He bends forward from the waist and says, "Well now and what has HE to do with this? Oh fuck's sake, I've work, good BYE!" He says the goodbye with his head; tilted left on the good and right on the bye, for real emphasis and, of course, for the last word he must have. She gives it to him and salutes him goodbye.

Now she takes off the dark glasses and leans back in the wooden chair with her feet on her desk, the dog in her lap, and his skinny little legs have stopped trembling. They share the rest of the sandwich, one bite for her, one for him.

CLOUDS AND COLD have moved back in on Cork. The bus from Kinsale swings wide into the Cork bus depot and stops with a hiss. Mary sits still inside the bus, looking over the crowd sitting along the station benches. The few people at the front of the bus take their bags from overhead compartments and get off.

The orange-haired boy from the back of the bus smiles at Mary as he walks by and says hello as he passes. Mary says hello back, then she nudges the old man across the aisle to wake up. He wakes slowly and smiles at Mary.

Outside the bus, in the cold, they say goodbye, with the old white-haired man doing a little bow to Mary, and with a tip of his cap, he wobbles off. In the other direction, the boy walks down the street, carrying his paperback book and a blue jean jacket over his shoulder. A tall boy, he walks in long strides, and the cold wind blows his orange hair back. He steps into a doorway, out of the wind.

There's an empty bench and Mary sits down. She got here a little sooner than she thought she would, and she wants to slow down and take in the moment, her first day in Cork. She pulls out the Cork pamphlet to check the hotel address again and look at the map. It's an easy walk along the river and a couple of side street detours over. She sits and looks around, takes her time.

There are new people here, pubs and restaurants and stores she's never been in and when she gets up and walks down the street she'll be somewhere she doesn't know at all, around every corner just that much more new. She doesn't know how she'll be able to sleep tonight.

People are smiling at her. She smiles back and takes a deep breath.

"I'm here!" she whispers to herself. Kinsale is only eighteen miles away, but it feels so far away to her now.

Mary stands up with her bags and starts walking down Merchant's Quay towards her hotel.

The orange-haired boy follows her.

HOLIDAY INN DREAMS

DECLAN O'SULLIVAN is setting up his new business in the middle of Cork, near the big mall. He's pacing around in his new-smelling office in his white sneakers and jeans and sweatshirt that says KILLARNEY across the front. He's popping open his boxes of files and papers and staplers and his brand-new computer equipment.

He stands in a corner of a room, drinking his takeaway coffee from the Starbucks downstairs, and wonders where he'll put his great large desk. He looks out the window. Yes, he thinks, that's it! I'll put the desk in the center of the window, facing back into the room, me facing the clients. Cork will be behind me as a dramatic backdrop as I guide them towards their dreams.

Declan puts his coffee on the floor and walks over to push the desk into place by the window. He inches it here and there, pushes a corner of the big desk back until it's square and centered. He lays out his new desk blotter and his black marble pen set with the small Irish flags flying in the center of the desk. He arranges the chairs around the desk.

Then he walks back to the other side of the room, picks up the coffee, and checks it all out. He imagines himself talking with his clients as the buildings rise behind his desk, behind him. He will use the view to dramatize his client's dreams of the future, to encourage them to think big for the future while they live small in the present, as he thinks he has successfully done.

This is so much better than the last job but the last job made this happen, he knows, and he's grateful. In the last job, he had an office, which he shared with another man. He had his own small radio and CD player on his desk, which he had to keep turned down low, and old, out-of-date computer equipment. There was a window with no view.

He looks with pride at his brand new white computer, big desk, and the view of Cork behind it.

"Thank you, father," he whispers to himself.

He had worked hard to become assistant manager of the Holiday Inn in Killarney. That had taken awhile, but he hadn't been able to make it above assistant manager. The other guy, the one he shared his office with, had. He was the manager. And the other guy had gotten married and then he had a baby, all this just after his promotion. And then the other guy was driving all over Ireland to motel seminars and tourism conventions with his new wife and baby while Declan ran the Holiday Inn.

And so Declan ran the Holiday Inn and when all the guests were in bed he'd log onto an internet finance class. His father was an investment counselor. Declan knew his father was a rich man, had his own firm, and so he started taking the online classes. He did nothing else but this and run the Holiday Inn and sleep in a room at the motel, near the office. It was off-season, and the motel was never more than half-full.

He didn't buy gas for his old college car because it never left the parking lot. His days were these things—the computer class, Holiday Inn paperwork and payroll routines, speaking with the desk clerks and sometimes the customers when there was a billing or reservation problem.

He would go into the motel pub after dinner and look at what few women were there. They were mostly businesswomen this time of year, so he knew he had a lot in common with many of them, being an investment counselor, almost. He wasn't *assistant manager* at night when he was in the pub. The bartender and waitress didn't give it away, either. And the motel manager, who was never there, never knew about it.

He would buy a drink for one of these women, usually one sitting alone at the bar. He would do many things— clap along with the trad music, buy the woman another drink, ask her what kind of business she was in, order them both food, listen to the woman talk about herself, loudly shout a request to the singer using his first name, signal the barman for another round, and describe what he thought of as the electric and even spiritual nature of investment counseling.

Of all these things the thing he did least well was listen to the woman talk to him.

He was passionate about investment counseling, though, as he would repeat as often as a fresh drink arrived, "Now don't be getting me wrong, um, what was your name again? ...yes, well, money isn't everything. No! No, no, no, don't be getting me wrong about that! I like to think of my job as more like Dream-weaving, you know what I mean? We all have dreams, but you need yarn to make the grand shawl of your life. I'm the yarn spinner! And like I always say, 'You have to be awake to make your inner dreams come true!'"

The barman watched Declan when he began doing this with the women because he hadn't seen this much life in the assistant manager in general. Or actually, never at all. Then, over that winter, he got used to it, brought the drinks, and stopped watching Declan.

Most of the women would feel at first bombarded, then cornered, eventually ignored, and finally bored with Declan. But sometimes he'd go back to the motel room with one of them. Always the woman's room. Never his room, which would give him away as night finance student, day motel assistant manager.

But it had all worked out after that long winter, and he'd passed the tests and gotten a certificate and a license and given notice to the manager and left the Holiday Inn and now here he stands in his new office.

His father had retired from his big investment firm in Dublin about the same day Declan had retired from the

Holiday Inn in Killarney, and he'd given him the money to rent the office space and buy the desk and chairs and the new computer equipment and the new black car downstairs. The money from his father had also covered his new apartment in Cork for a year, covering him until he "gets on his feet."

Declan wishes his father could be here with him on his first day in his new office and help arrange the chairs with him and put the art on the wall. He knows his father would like where he's put the desk. He remembers well his father's desk and his office in Dublin looking out over the River Liffey.

Declan wishes his father was here now. But his father and mother are on a long sea cruise with friends.

Declan puts the coffee down on his desk and picks up a framed sign. He looks around his office, then decides on the place to hang it, behind his desk near the window.

YOU HAVE TO BE AWAKE TO MAKE
YOUR INNER DREAMS COME TRUE!

He looks out the window on the busy morning street. He pulls his big black chair over to the window so he can watch the people and drink his coffee. He smiles.

"I'm going to wake you all up," he says.

HOME OR SOMEWHERE LIKE

CHESTER STEPS out into the street, the sun has gone above the clouds and it's cold. He looks right, down the street, then left up the other way, and chooses left, uphill, to start walking. He needs to pee badly, then another drink, badly. He needs to get home, or somewhere.

He watches the edge of the sidewalk for a guiding line along the street, and he whistles a song for the appearance of not being as drunk as he is.

Looking down at the sidewalk as he walks there are many shuffling shoes and trash, and then he stops and looks up over the rooftops of Cork, looking for his stone house on top of the hill. He finds it, and the small window he'd look down from this morning.

He begins to feel the crummy shameful bad feeling again, leaking into and filling up his brain. He hears music coming from the open door of Mother's Pub, and through the door he sees Mother. She's standing, leaning an elbow against the bar, in a white lacy blouse and a long red skirt touching black boots. Long yellow-white hair swirling down to her hips, which she's got cocked away from the bar. She yells out at him, flinging her hair with the yelling.

"Chester! Come over here! You stand there like you need a wee and a rest and a drink! Or like you were carryin' the very weight of the world on your wee—speakin' of wee—shoulders!"

And so he smiles again, and abandons the sidewalk edge and the whistling and normalcy again for sitting down and talking or not talking in the warm of Mother's Pub. In he goes, as his stone house sits up on the hill and watches over him and Cork through that window.

Later, afternoon light fading outside the pub windows, Chester sits alone in the backroom watching Mother clowning with several laughing patrons. Chester feels drunk now as if he were two miles down in the ocean. He sits figuring out how to get the money laid out to pay for his drinks, then gets to the door without embarrassment, and then gets home and into his bed.

And just then, an old, strong hand with white hair coming out the coat sleeve squeezes his shoulder.

"Come on, Chester." It's Kieran. Kieran runs an inn out beyond Cork near the airport and it's called Kieran's Inn. He was the first man Chester met straight from the airport, middle of the night, candlelighting the way up the stairs of the inn to a lovely, wood-beamed top-floor room. Chester, not drunk that night but tired after the jet trip from the United States to London and then back to Ireland, had staggered to and fumbled about at the front desk of Kieran's Inn, looking for his credit card and his reservation papers he'd made over the internet. Kieran, in a red flannel nightshirt and his shaggy and night-messed white hair up in the air, only laughed softly, kindly, and squeezed Chester by the shoulder.

"Let's get you upstairs and into bed, shall we? We'll leave off all that shit 'til breakfast, OK with you?" Chester looked at this warm old white-haired man, a broad red face with deep wrinkles in the brow and eyes from years of laughter and smiling, and saw something he'd been really looking for and needing.

Going up the stairs, the flickering shadows of the candle Kieran carried along the narrow stairwell, and the creaking of the wooden steps. Kieran placing his bags in a corner of the room and flicking on the bathroom light so as to not blind the weary traveler, five minutes from a deep sleep. Chester staring at the bed, which looked wonderful and safe after more than twenty-four hours of bus and taxi and airport and hours over the ocean and airport and inspections and bright overhead lights and loudspeakers.

Turning to the old man, a silhouette in the doorway holding up the candle to illuminate his face, the old man saying, "Goodnight son. Sleep well and long. In the morning it'll be tea or a pint, depending! Welcome to Ireland." The door shutting with a secure thump and the heavy steps back downstairs. The front door to the inn locked with many solid clicks.

Chester lying down into that bed for good, long hours of peace in the safe warm dark.

And now, as then, the hand on Chester's shoulder. Kieran raising him up and out of the back booth and the black funk and paying his tab with Mother. On the way out, Mother breaks off from the customers to kiss Chester on the cheek and the forehead and hug him. And the customers, not to be left out of any kind of local love, interrupt their own stories and lies and surround Kieran and Mother and Chester, mostly Chester. And Chester, who'd thought he couldn't talk to anyone today now wants to but can't with all the shouting and toasting of him by the customers. Mother and Kieran watch this for awhile until some ease comes back into Chester's face and then they wink at each other, kiss each other, and begin to break it all up. Kieran gets Chester out the front door of Mother's Pub, all the customers waving and toasting and falling down and some of them trying to go home with them.

Just a few minutes later, in Kieran's van (the van that has "Kieran's Inn Shuttle Van" very officially painted in green capital letters on the back and along the sides), Chester watches his house go by in the twilight, then looks straight ahead down the road in the lowering fog. Kieran turns on his headlights. Chester turns and watches his house fade away. The old hand comes down on his knee.

"Need a bit of help in the mornin', caseloads comin' down from Dublin in trucks first thing and then the electrical man comin' in to fix the wiring in the speakers in the bar and I'm not going to handle it all at once alone." A pause from Kieran, then the big smile flashing in the dashboard light. "Hope you don't mind too much, old son." And then, the chuckling again.

Chester slides down and relaxes in his seat. He feels in his pants pocket his keys and knows his house is safe for the night back there. He lets that go. And he knows Rob will get home all right as well, living only a few doors down and across the street from the pub.

Kieran drives the shuttle van fast through the turns and hills and fog and flicks on the defroster as the windows mist over.

The road curves down out of the hills and levels out and the pale yellow lights of Kieran's Inn glow out of the night and the fog. And above, the blinking red and blue lights of a jet coming down out of the fog for a landing at the airport. Chester relaxes and fades into sleep.

Kieran slows down and coasts into the gravel lot of the Inn and stops. He shuts off the engine and the lights and the van backfires and Chester is awake again.

"I must fix that," Kieran says.

The inn is dark, and Kieran opens his van door a crack letting in the cold night air and the trickling water sound of a creek nearby.

"Fish in that stream yonder, you know. Maybe we get breakfast there one day sometime soon we aren't so busy." The old man looks down at the dashboard and turns off the light that his open door has turned on, and he sighs.

Kieran elbows Chester in the side. "Let's go on in and pass out." They get out of the van and walk up on the porch and into the front hall in the dark. Kieran shuts and locks the front door and turns around to face Chester. They stand together in the dark, the yellow light from the neon sign outside shining across their faces. Kieran smiles at Chester.

"See you in the mornin' then, Chester. You take that room on the top floor again tonight. It's unlocked, just walk on up and I'll see you in the a.m. Not early, though. You just sleep in and we'll see. We'll get it all done, won't we?"

They shake hands and Chester goes up the stairs to a good, long night of peaceful sleep in the safe, warm, dark.

THE HAPPY IDIOT

ROB GETS HOME and shuts the door behind him. He drops his keys in the empty coffee can at the foot of the front door, and throws shut the lock and latch. He rubs his cold red hands. All these different and routine nightly sounds bring out his little grey cat. Rob goes into the kitchen and creaks open the old white refrigerator and brings out the milk bottle. Rob pours the milk into a yellow bowl with ALEX painted on it. Then he gets out the one more cold bottle of ale he'd left himself for when he got home.

"One drink, Alex, then to bed." He says this every night and then sits on the floor with his cat, his coat still on, both of them sitting and drinking, in the light of the open refrigerator door.

Rob lies in bed with Alex sleeping by his head, purring, thinks Rob, like a sewing machine. He smiles in the dark listening to the purring and the rain and remembering the singing in the pub today. He falls asleep and has a dream of his father that wakes him. Rob gets up, puts on an old red and black checkered robe, and goes to the window. He looks down the street at Shane's Pub, closed and dark. A car comes down the road, wipers sloshing back and forth, and passes by. He starts thinking about his father calling him the "Happy Idiot" as a nickname when he was a baby. He was a happy baby no matter what, his mother had told him, laughing and smiling no matter what was going on. And so they gave the nickname. And they had called him by that nickname still, the last time he'd seen his mother and father, ten years ago, in Waterford.

He remembers that day as he looks out the window to the rainy street.

Rob had come to the Waterford glass factory for his father's retirement party. He had bought a new green suit and a new brown tie and he had come to watch his father retire. Night after night before the party, he'd stayed up late at his kitchen table with ballpoint pens and pads of paper writing a speech to give his father. Ballpoint pens, pads of paper, can after can of ale, and his Beatles records playing to make him more creative, he thought. And he wrote far into the night.

Rob remembers walking up to the factory on the day of the retirement party in his new suit and the speech in his inside breast pocket. He'd noticed his parent's car in the lot as he came up the hill to the factory from the bus stop, and it was ok with him that they had come straight here without picking him up. He knew they would be nervous about the special day, and *not* thinking about him, so Rob came on his own.

He went inside the Waterford building, into the men's toilet to check how he looked. He straightened his tie and wiped the rain off his shoulders and smiled at himself in the bathroom mirror. He pulled out his speech to make sure all the pages were there (and *in order)* for reading, and then walked back into the hallway.

And there, down at the end of the hallway, he saw his father and mother surrounded by all his father's friends and co-workers. Rob's sister was there with her husband and three children. They were all moving together towards a door into the big auditorium where the speeches, including Rob's, would be made. Rob's father looked down the hall and saw Rob. He stopped and looked at Rob and the crowd stopped laughing and talking and looked at Rob, too.

Rob remembers now that he gave a little wave, or salute, to his father.

And his father, seeing this, had smiled at his son, pointed down the hall, and proudly said to his friends, "Ladies and Gentlemen, my son, the Happy Idiot. My unemployed son, that is. I'll say one thing for him, he retired even earlier than I did!"

There was loud laughter at that remark and Rob had even smiled back down the hall at his father and mother and the friends as they moved into the auditorium. Then he walked the other way, down the hallway in the other direction. He'd gotten lost for a few minutes in the halls of the glass factory but kept on walking, taking an elevator down, coming out into another hallway, and at last coming out on a shipping and receiving dock, where he jumped down and ran into a wet field beyond the factory.

He ran back to the bus stop but continued on along the road until he got to his apartment a mile outside of Waterford. He rushed inside, shut the door hard behind him, and locked it. He sat down at his kitchen table and looked at all the ballpoint pens and pads of paper and then he was up and pacing. He walked a line from the kitchen through the hall to his tiny bedroom and then back again, looking out the kitchen window each time. Nobody was ever out there.

He put on a Beatles record, *Abbey Road*, nearly breaking it on the turntable, and turned the volume all the way up. He kept pacing back and forth, looking out the window each time. A knocking on the front door turned into a pounding on the front door and then the landlord came in holding his large ring of keys. The landlord walked into the apartment and turned off the music. Rob watched as the landlord looked around the room at papers on the table and floor, empty beer and wine bottles everywhere.

"I'll give you a week," the landlord said. "You're paid up to date for last month but I'll give you a week and I'll give your deposit back. I don't see you working lately, maybe that'll get you through until you get work." The landlord looked at Rob once more and stepping over the bottles, left the apartment, shutting the door softly.

Rob didn't want to be there another week.

That night, Rob remembers, he was on the bus, still in his brown suit and green tie, his speech still in his pocket, watching the glass factory pass by and fade behind the bus in the dark. He turned and watched it go by, looked back that way for a good long while, then watched the light of Waterford itself disappear. He was riding west, towards Cork, and he had his apartment deposit with him. He had this money, and he had his Beatles records in a box on the seat next to him. He left the pads and pens and bottles for his father's speech back in the apartment. And Rob, sitting in the front seat near the bus driver, looked ahead down the road, no idea what to do next.

Tonight, Rob looks down the street towards Shane's Pub where he has his regular table with his new friend Chester. The bartender, Tommy, is also becoming a friend. Rob pulls the curtains shut and turns to look at his cat, curled in the bed and sleeping by his pillow. He takes off his robe and lays it around Alex as a sort of flannel nest, and gets back into bed. Sleepy now, he eases his head into the pillow, closes his eyes, and listens to the rain outside in the street.

"Fuckin' right, Dah," he says. "Happy idiot. That's me."

READY OR NOT, HERE COMES SOMETHING

TOMMY IS ALONE and closing the pub. He has locked the front door and now he's lining up the cigar boxes to close out the cash and charge card receipts. He turns around and looks at the room. The pub windows are fogged up and cold. He looks across the barroom, the tables and chairs all messed around, and he remembers the day. He walks out into the pub, sits down in a corner booth.

Tommy looks back at his office behind the bar, the only lighted area of the pub. He looks at that for a long few minutes. He thinks that this is really where he will be tomorrow and the next day and the next day and the next day. He wonders if he'll ever be able to sing again above a whisper. Tomorrow, back to normal, he thinks.

No one would be looking for him to be singing, they would not want it. No one even knows he wants to, except maybe Rob. Tommy, filling up with this thinking, gets up again and goes to lock up the cigar boxes beneath the bar, and he pulls on his coat. The radio's on and he pours one last small beer. He sings with the radio, and reads the note he'd written to himself this morning.

There's a sharp rap on the front door. There's some movement out there through the fogged-up front door window. Someone standing out there in the dark, in sunglasses. He walks over, squinting to see through the door, and unlocks it.

He knows this woman in a green corduroy coat and red-framed dark sunglasses who's got such a large smile for him, and red lipstick on this late. She's come in here before, always alone, always with the sunglasses on. Tommy thinks that he's never seen her eyes. She's got a little pepper-colored dog with her. The dog looks up at him, puffing little puffs of breath in the cold air, then shakes his head, slapping his ears on the sides of his head.

"Hello Tommy," she says.

"Hello. Sorry, don't know your name..."

"Sondra. I saw the light and thought I heard singing as well. Was that you? Anyway, I just thought I'd say hello. I know your name from your friend Rob. He got his little cat from the shelter and I asked about you one day."

Tommy isn't wet but suddenly he feels like he did that night at sea. He says nothing but he's looking into those dark glasses, looking for her eyes.

Sondra shrugs her shoulders and laughs with her big smile again. Up on her toes, she kisses Tommy on the cheek, shrugs again, and says "Good night, Tommy!" She clicks her mouth at the little dog, and they leave.

Tommy stands in the pub door watching Sondra walk away. She's got long legs in purple leggings and she's walking very slowly and—*fluidly*—that's the word, he thinks. He wonders how she can walk like that or see where she's going with those dark glasses on. He watches those long, slow strides until she's out of sight. Then he listens to the tinkling of the dog leash until it fades away. It's cold out in the street. The tops of the buildings have disappeared in the fog. The streetlights are misty and fuzzy and yellow.

Tommy walks back inside the pub, shuts and locks the front door, and stands there a moment. Then he walks back through the pub without bumping into anything at all, shuts off the back bar lights, turns off the radio, finishes the small beer, goes out through the back door, locks it, and walks down the alley, going home. He'll be there in ten minutes. He'll be in bed five minutes after that. He's gotten used to this.

But as he walks home through the mist he's not sleepy. In ten minutes he comes to his door but passes by and keeps walking.

It's cold, it's late and already tomorrow, but it's not going to be back to normal.

NEPO

IN THE DARKNESS, there's a tinkling sound along the River Lee but it's nothing to do with boats or pissing.

Sondra walks along with her new friend on the leash. She's trying to come up with a name for him, and being as wide awake as she is, having just kissed Tommy, this is the night. She's reading street signs, the names of bars and stores, she's stopped and read each statue she's come across, she's looked at the names on the churches but she doesn't want to name the dog Father something or Saint somebody else.

Sondra walks into a pool of yellow light on the wet street and looks up at the yellow and brown Guinness sign glowing in the rain. She looks down and another sign says OPEN, and she clicks to the dog to follow her into the pub.

She walks into very faint light in the pub, her eyes going right away to the brightest light in the room, a square of bright light which is the soccer game on the flat-screen TV at the end of the bar. A bartender stands under the screen alone, watching the game. Her eyes adjusting in the dark pub, a table of men to her right comes into focus. They are not watching the soccer, a couple of them are barely upright in their chairs, and one of them has his head down on the table and he's the one talking.

"Rain, rain, rain, rain, rain, rain, rain, rain," he's saying into the tabletop. "I fuckin' love the rain. Which one of you fuckers told me they'd have to pour me into my grave? Well, you were fucking right about that. Mine will be a watery grave someone said." He is still face down but he has a finger up in the air making this point.

"I don't think they were referring to the rain, Eddy, but fair play to you," one of the other men says, then looks up and smiles at Sondra. The dog starts shaking off the rain, spraying water across the table and waking up the ones slumped down in their chairs. One of them looks down at the dog and stands up. He takes his hat off for Sondra.

"Who's this one, miss?"

Sondra smiles at him and at the table. They all wonder how she's getting around in those sunglasses. One of the men whispers to the one next to him, "Poor thing ... blind."

"Well, that's my problem tonight, gents. I just got him today and I still haven't named him. He's a stray. Doesn't seem right him not having a name and so I've been walking around all night racking my brain over a name. And I tell you, I'm stuck."

The table is still and silent. The man with his face on the table has straightened up in his chair. This, clearly, is important business. The bartender has turned off the TV and was walking to the table to close up but as he gets near the silent table, he stops. He's thinking. The man who has stood up and taken his hat off to Sondra puts his hat back on suddenly.

"Sit down, miss, sit down. Come, let's all have another round, um, do you mind James? She needs a name for this wee stray dog, we need one more round of drinks to think, then we're off, alright? One more, on me, you too James, you pour one for yourself, then we're off to home, alright?"

James the bartender looks down at the dog and walks back to the bar. Halfway back to the bar he stops and turns around. They all look at him. He has an idea already.

"My mother-in-law, my *rich* mother-in-law, she moved to a fancy apartment in Dublin, doorman and all, and her doorman's name was 'Dragon.' How's that?" The table is silent again for a moment then suddenly noisy with the men throwing around their own ideas for a name. James continues on to the bar for a tray of drinks, still thinking.

Sondra sits at the head of the table and watches these men frantically trying to come up with a name, arguing, looking around the room for inspiration, one of them taking out a large, beat-up plastic cell phone, tries to call someone, gives up and keeps thinking. The nameless dog sits in her lap, also watching the men. Sondra looks down into his face.

"Where were you last night?" The dog looks up at her, licks her, then watches the men again with his ears up and his head cocked to the side. They all have ideas.

"My brother named his dog Yeats, after the poet."

"Too pretentious. How about naming him after a drink? Maybe she could call him Beamish. Or Guinness."

"Not enough dignity. I like the poet idea. But maybe Oscar Wilde instead of Yeats. Just Oscar. Or Seamus Heaney, shortened to Seamus. Or Heaney. Brendan Behan. Take your choice between Brendan or Behan."

"That's not bad, but let's make it more modern. Oh, I have it! Ready? BONO. I like that. It's dignified but more current."

"I don't know, I don't know," they're all saying, not ready to settle yet. James comes back with the tray and it gets quiet again as they all sip their drinks.

Rain sprays across the window in a blast of wind and one of the men looks out there through the window into the night. This one, the one who had his face down on the table a few minutes ago, is suddenly very focused and the others see it. They wait for him to say something. Then he says something.

"Nepo."

Sondra looks over her shoulder, through the window where he's looking.

"Again William? What was that? *Nero?*"

"Nepo."

They all look down at the dog. Sondra looks down too. He looks back at them, up at her. She whispers to him.

"Nepo?" His tail starts wagging and the men all laugh. They raise their glasses and James the barman stands up.

"To NEPO!" And they all toast. The dog, Nepo, tries to jump up on the table. Sondra is smiling but looking over her shoulder through the window again to where "Nepo" came from. Something *out there*, she thinks.

"I like it," she says.

"Sounds kind of nautical to me," says another. I'm not a navy man though I do know about port and starboard and fore and aft, but wasn't there something about Nepo as well? A constellation to be guided by at sea, maybe?"

"No, no. It's a God ain't it, William? Greek or Roman, one or the other. The God of Rain or something."

"No, it's a mountain or a holy shrine in the middle east somewhere or something, right William? Mount Nepo?"

William is face down on the table again, but smiling. They'll have to help him home now, but he has accomplished something tonight, he knows. They all know it.

The men get up from the table, shake hands with each other, shake hands with Sondra, they all pet Nepo, then help William out into the night. James tells Sondra to take her time, finish her drink, he still has some closing-up things to do.

She likes the name but still does not understand where it's come from. It's a name she's surely heard before. She thinks back through her literature classes at Trinity College but nothing comes of that.

Lights are being turned off one by one in the bar, so she stands up, takes her drink over to the window. She looks out the window and the rain is easing some.

There are white stars sharp and clear in the sky over the dark rolling river.

There are little bugs buzzing around the orange neon letters of the OPEN sign in the window and then it is switched off by James. It's time to go. Sondra takes a last long swallow of stout, yawns, and buttons her coat.

"Nepo, ready?" The dog is wagging and ready. Sondra stops and smiles, turns around back to the window. She starts to laugh.

"I wasn't drunk enough to see it, little friend. Little Nepo!"

She is looking through the letters of the OPEN sign, facing out into the street.

IT'S LATE NOW IN CORK, and only a few yellow lights glow along the streets below if you're looking down on the city from the hills above. On one edge of town, you can see the one last-lit pub sign advertising stout, then it goes out. You just hear the wind. The wind has flown into town and blown away the fog and the rain now that most everyone's asleep, and the yellow streetlights flicker inside the trees blowing back and forth down below.

Underneath the pub sign that just went out, you hear someone crash out through the door, and then you see him stumble up the street, elbows and knees at wildly different angles. There's the sound of singing and a bottle dropping, rolling into the street, stopping with a clink on the curb. A few moments of footsteps in the dark, and another door locks with a sharp click echoing up the hill to where you're standing, watching, listening.

And the wind, which has stopped a moment for this straggler, comes back over the hill through the leaves and down into Cork again. You just hear the leaves and the wind.

You look down on the windows, all the dark squares under the hills and stars. Whatever hard things may have happened inside those squares today; hard words shot back and forth and around in those rooms, or no words whatsoever at all, everything and everyone in those dark rooms is now in agreement. No longer the time for worrying about the permanently asleep days and years past. No longer the time for figuring things out and planning ahead to get ahead to get control to avoid trouble.

No longer the time for trying to control the wind that comes every night anyway.

There's dreaming going on down there, maybe some bad dreaming going on down there too, but the day is ended and that's something to have in common. It's a start.

On nights like this, this is what you might be thinking. On nights like this, with a certain kind of music in your head, you might not want to go to bed at all. You think you'll go walking down every one of those streets you see below, and you'll look in every window and write a note for each house to find in the morning, on the front door, an answer, this piece of peace you're feeling tonight. Every front door gets your note in the morning because they should have been on the hill with you tonight seeing what you saw. Whatever it was.

But, of course, being just another one, you'll go home and go to bed too. You couldn't have really written it down anyway. But for awhile longer, you'll stand up here and be still. The yellow streetlights blink in the waving trees below and you know you haven't far to go to get home. You'll get there, easy.

There's no other sound now but the sound of the wind blowing through Cork and into its windows and under its doors and covering the town like a blanket.

Some down there below are asleep and dreaming.

Some are wide awake and dreaming.

EVERYTHING THEY KNEW
AND EVERYTHING NEW

MARY WAKES UP and there's a new ceiling above her!

She gets out of bed and walks out into the hall, looking down the stairs towards the reception desk and dining room. There are hands down there holding a newspaper at the reception desk, but no face above it, blocked by the stair rail.

She looks down the hall and the young man from the bus is teetering and naked, and as he turns to focus on Mary, he points to her very specifically and accurately and without using what he usually uses to point with.

Mary looks down and her eyes have focused on something.

"Good morning to you," she says. "I'd say *Rise and Shine,* but I see you already have."

The young man doesn't seem to know yet what she means, and then he hears laughter from below, from downstairs, where there's now a curious smiling face leaning forward into view from behind the morning paper at the desk.

"Good mornin', Eric," says the kind and amused face downstairs, leaning back out of sight behind the paper. Eric peers down there trying to see who *this* is who knows his name. All he can see is the paper.

He turns and looks down the hall at the artwork on the walls. Along the walls between the doors are small paintings of flowers and tea cups and one of a green hillside and blue sky with a white cottage, all of them lit by small lights in the ceiling. He's fixed on these paintings, then on the wallpaper, which is deep dark red, with shiny embossed lions heads in a repeating pattern. He reaches out and touches the wallpaper and feels that it's a kind of rough velvet. He brushes the mat back and forth with his hand, his head leaning on the wall, seemingly holding him up.

He straightens up and walks to the painting of the cottage on the hillside. This simple house makes him smile, and he says softly aloud, "Ah, there it is, there's the place to be." He stands there swaying a bit, *gazing himself* into the cottage. He gazes himself in there with a writer's table by the window, and he gazes breakfast cooking in the kitchen on the other side of the cottage, facing the hillside. He gazes a beautiful girlfriend he doesn't have into the other window in the painting, which is the bedroom. She's still in bed. She lies there in white sheets half awake, eyes closed but smiling, the back of her freckled fingers lightly brushing her white thighs under the sheets.

Mary watches. The man downstairs puts down his paper and watches.

Eric moves closer into the bedroom in the painting. And as he moves even closer, trying to walk right into this dream life, he drives his erection straight into the wall below the painting.

"Fuck! Ow! Shit!"

Eric didn't want to disturb his girl in the sheets, but he woke her and himself with his own shouting.

He looks down and notices that he's naked. The newspapers rustle again downstairs as Eric runs down the hall into his room, slamming the door.

Mary looks down at the man at the desk.

"Good morning, Phillip."

"Mary. Bit of breakfast before the interview? Courage and sustenance?"

Mary looks down at him; she likes Phillip's smile.

"Be down in a few minutes."

Back in her room, Mary takes a slow and luxurious shower. She has the window open and she's having a good time mixing the cold foggy air outside with the steamy air inside.

She's taking a long shower, taking her time with the soap and washing her hair, getting ready for her appointment. This will be her first job interview in twenty-five years. But she's got a couple of hours and she feels really fine. Her new dress is laid out on the bed, and the new red shoes she brought from Kinsale are at the foot of the bed, waiting for their first walk. Mary has placed them just at a certain angle at the foot of the bed, and they look ready to go.

Mary looks out the shower window at her first morning in Cork. Across the alley from the hotel is the rear of a low building full of little stores, all the rear doors open and busy with light and men carrying boxes inside. Steam puffs out the top of the building through a row of chimneys and there are as many cats in the alley as men.

It all looks very cheerfully busy to Mary.

The warm soap rinses down her back and she watches the men work below, the graffiti in the alley looks like good art, and it all looks like her new neighborhood. She hopes so.

Back in his room, Eric paces around, in and out of the bathroom, around the bed, looking out the window, turns on and off the TV set, he is waking up at last. "Fuckin' hell" he keeps saying over and over, remembering the old lady next door and his dick sticking out in the hall and some guy downstairs knowing his first name.

He remembers the faces of the woman and the guy downstairs and he laughs a little. He feels better, remembering those two. Neither of them had given him the sour end-of-the-world-disappointed look he'd run from, and *that* was a first.

Eric goes to the window and pulls back the curtains, sits on the windowsill looking at the Cork skyline. He thinks about that disappointed look that he's used to, how it's held him tight and held him down.

Until now.

Born in Limerick, Eric lived there until a few days ago when he finally took off and away from his family for Kinsale. He'd been walking around late one night last week through his broken-window neighborhood, and walked by the window of a travel office. There was a picture of the bay and harbor at Kinsale and he decided he'd go there. When he told his family the idea he was immediately interrogated—*Why? What would he do there? Who gave him this idea? What next?*

It was always like this for Eric. With neither of his parents having any ideas for him or about him, no direction for him, no interest in him beyond *did you do anything wrong today?* he looked around everywhere for anything, anything he could do. He'd be a doctor, no—a soccer player. Maybe a cook, but no, even better—a barman! He'd go to the movies and on the walk home decide definitely on acting, but when he brought the idea up it disappeared even before his parent's laughter had died down.

And after the laughter, there was that sad, disappointed look again, his mother with tears in her eyes, the father saying his usual line.

"What next, son?"

What was next was leaving.

Eric had done it after the end of his dishwasher job a couple of days ago. He'd been working at a little restaurant at the Limerick bus station. His lunch shift over, he changed out of his wet, greasy dishwasher whites and back into his jeans and jacket. He picked up a small pack with books and clothes and a map of Kinsale and said "see you tomorrow" to his boss. The boss asked him about the pack and Eric told him it was laundry. Then he crossed the bus station parking lot, out of sight of the cafe, and got on the bus for Kinsale.

This was his first bus trip, his first trip anywhere, his first time out of Limerick. His family had no car, they all just walked around inside Limerick—mostly inside their own neighborhood—inside Limerick.

Out on the road, out of town, everything new, Eric watched everything he knew fade away behind him from the back seat window of the bus. He took out his wallet and counted his saved-up dishwashing money and there wasn't very much.

He didn't know how long the money would last. He knew nothing about Kinsale beyond the picture he'd seen that one night. He didn't want to know more than that and he hadn't brought up Kinsale again with anyone after his parents had laughed and shot down the idea.

No one knew he was going, that he was gone already. And when Eric looked back, Limerick was gone. He saw green hills rolling away and clouds lowering like a blanket over what was behind him.

The bus was going fast around the curves and he felt he was going fast and out of control in the same way, and it scared him and thrilled him and he'd never felt scared or thrilled. Behind him the sky was coming down low and ahead, looking down the aisle of the bus and out the front windshield, the sky looked nearly black and it was starting to rain. His thoughts and feelings were as wild as the speeding bus and the violent sky. And he was smiling. He was out of control, out of Limerick, no notion what was ahead.

He winked at his reflection in the bus window.

Eric had never felt so much electricity in his body or such clearness in his head, but then he thought of his mother weeping back in the little house and his father walking around hitting walls and doors, and trying to console her. This deadened him for a moment or so, and he felt mean about what he was doing to them, but the bus was going very fast. There was no stopping this.

Eric decided to *un-deaden* himself. He decided not to have his brain sucked back to Limerick through the back window of the bus, his body to follow. This is the way he did it. He'd make a list, the list would be short, it would be three things, and he knew the three:

1. From the very beginning his parents had looked at him like he was making life sad for them.

2. With no advice or encouragement from them, he came up with the ideas, and they laughed or ignored them all.

3. He graduated from high school over a year ago and had been working as a dishwasher at the bus station since the ceremony.

The list was made in his head, then he wrote it all down in the first person point of view (his!), and his frown disappeared. He didn't look out the back window anymore.

"So be it," he said. "Fuck them. I tried, they didn't, I waited, for nothing, so fuck them." And the bus drove fast towards Kinsale, into the rain.

The first night in Kinsale, Eric took a room looking out over the harbor. He had a drink downstairs in the hotel pub, then brought a bag of stout up to the room and set the cans on the outside ledge of the window to cool them in the night air and rain, and he sat and watched the harbor and the streets below.

He'd walked those streets after checking into the hotel, looking for places where he might work. There were loads of restaurants, and he could be a dishwasher in any of them. Knowing this had given Eric some peace as he sat in his window gazing out over the tops of the buildings. And he decided to slow down and feel what it's like, the night in a new unknown town.

Eric feels a bit of peace again this morning remembering all of this, sitting on another windowsill in Cork, though he is looking out over this city, with less money and no job.

But it's as alright with Eric this morning as it was that night in Kinsale. He's already learned something.

Nothing planned and the money running out and in a place he's never been before is better than waiting in Limerick with all those long years of long faces and long memories and short imaginations.

Eric stayed in that hotel window all night in Kinsale. He'd been awake for two days, but he didn't care. He drank the rain-cooled beer and watched the rain come and stop and start again. The beer mixed with no sleep for two days mixed with leaving home mixed with this room in a town he'd never been in and knowing nobody here at all was getting him very high. He watched the streets below his room for hours and saw no one and then someone would come along, walking to who knows where. He watched lights go off and on in little windows in Kinsale and wondered what the people inside them were like. He sat in the window and thought about all of his life living in one town, on the same street, inside the same apartment, the same things said over and over.

It was expected he wouldn't do anything much different.

Eric's conversations in that apartment having to do with dreams or *something else* ended in frowning and tears and then the silence came back over the apartment, except for the sound of the TV set, always on.

When he saw a few more people walking below he knew dawn was coming. There was a light blue line in the sky over the hill of houses. He was especially fond of the older men and women hustling along down there. He admired these older men and women up awake and dressed in the cold and dark, puffing and clomping along to work with what seemed like happy energy—*work to go to!* He was thinking that they didn't walk along like prisoners because they were old or had to go to work. And what Eric heard below in the dark was certainly hard breathing, even wheezing, but not sighing. This was new to Eric. And they were saying hello to each other in loud, distinctly happy voices like it was the afternoon! This was also new to Eric. He was used to waking up in silence, everybody looking at the floor, coming home later to the same.

The blue line on the hill was filling out now into pink sky under the clouds and he was hearing people in the hall of his hotel now. Getting lighter and busier outside, he opened his last can of beer. He opened it and toasted Kinsale. A man below heard the can open and looked up. He smiled at Eric and yelled up at him.

"There you go! Good way to start the day! Fair play to you!" He was a short husky man in a long blue wool coat and thick grey uncombed hair flying back and he was still laughing as he walked fast around a corner and out of sight. Eric held his can up as a toast to him until he couldn't hear the laughing anymore. Funny thing too, because he had tried at first to hide the can when he saw the man look up.

Again, something new.

Eric found the piece of paper on which he'd written the list of his life in Limerick, and then took up his pen to add something.

I'm a hider, he wrote. I'm used to hiding.

He put his shoes on and put all the empty beer cans in a bag for the maid. His coat on, he looked out the window once more before leaving the room. A small round woman in a red sweater and a black hat was walking down the street. He laughed because he thought her colors were like a ladybug, but she wasn't walking like one. She seemed to be on the way to something. Like the others he was admiring from his window, he liked this woman too. He watched her a little longer. It was something about the hat. Then, she went around the corner.

Eric went downstairs to the front desk to pay for his night and no one was there. He rang the bell; nobody came. He walked down a little hall and into the small kitchen, lights were on, nobody here either. He went back out to the desk. Then he sat down in a big green wingback chair in the lobby across from the desk and looked at the paintings on the wall. He started laughing again, nobody around to pay, and then the front door flew open, and it was the man who'd yelled up at him from the street. The man stopped a moment, saw Eric, and broke into a big smile and laugh. He came over and shook hands with Eric.

"How was the beer?" And he was laughing again, walking to the desk. "Another night or are you on your way?" He slammed down his satchel on the desk and looked at Eric.

"Looks like you're on your way to me." Eric still hadn't said anything. "But the place is nearly empty, so if you change your mind, come back. Glad to have you."

Eric opened his wallet and the man watched him count his money.

"This is *really* off-season, I never make money this time of year, so why don't we call it half the usual, ok son?" Eric looked up from his wallet. The man was leaning forward on the desk and smiling at him.

"I keep it open this time of year as my office, my own pub, a place to be with my friends, pretend that I'm working, do some drinking, and be host to adventurers like you."

Eric gave him some money and they shook hands.

"I don't know if I'll stay another night or not, I thought I'd just go out and walk around a bit, see the town." This was maybe the longest sentence Eric had said in two days and he worried about how he sounded to the innkeeper, but the man was warmly smiling at him, so he went on.

"I don't really know where I'm going," he said, and the man waved this off with a snort.

"Neither do I, son, neither do I." The man left the desk suddenly and went down the hall. He returned with two mugs of what was mostly coffee and gave one to Eric.

"You'll find this thing about knowing where you're going doesn't matter much. I'm a Catholic, but the Buddhists have this clever fuckin' thing about paying attention to where you are in the moment at hand as being much more to the point, you know? I bet you're doing fine."

The two were quiet for a few moments and sipped the mostly coffee.

"My name's Jim."

"Eric." And they shook hands for the third time. Jim stared at Eric a moment. Then he seemed to decide something.

"Eric, you know that half you just gave me? Let's halve it again," and he handed Eric back some money. "Go see the town, the countryside. Maybe Cork. That's where I'm from, and I love it here, here I'll stay, but maybe you should try Cork. It's a bit louder there, you might say. You should give it a look."

Eric put the money back in his wallet and felt a little shaky.

"You're welcome here anytime, Eric."

Jim came around the desk and they walked out the front door into the street and stood in front of the hotel. A young red-headed girl in black boots and green woolen stockings walked past them and said good morning. Jim squeezed Eric on the shoulder.

"I'll see you later tonight or next week or in five years, Eric. Come back anytime, my friend. And if it is tonight, you can bring *her* too!"

Jim started laughing again and went back inside his hotel. Eric walked away down the street, towards the harbor and the bus depot.

When he got to the depot, he saw the little ladybug woman with the black hat and red sweater again. She sat on a bench, her tongue stuck out at something. Eric looked across the street and saw what she was sticking it out at— the Starbucks shop. There was a car on the street in front of the woman and the driver was giving the Starbucks shop the finger.

Eric thought that there was certainly something about this woman and the way she was wearing her hat.

Eric looked back once more at Kinsale. He could hear water sloshing in the harbor but when he looked at buildings or faces they seem to tilt and shift.

He looked at the woman with the hat, sitting and waiting for the bus. He had been trying to focus on something still so that *he* could get still and think for a moment, and then he heard the bus. The bus said Cork on the front. He ran to the depot, bought a ticket, and got back to the bus just in time to get on, the last one on before the driver shut the door. He looked at the woman as he passed by on the way to the back of the bus.

She was gazing out the window. He wondered if he looked like she did, two people getting free of something. That's how she looked to Eric.

He sat down in the back of the bus and he was off again, feeling out of control, going somewhere again.

Eric remembers everything glowing and golden and fuzzy and tilting on that morning. It had been two days and no sleep and drinking all night. And now, here in Cork, it's a new day and still he hasn't slept. He can smell sausage cooking downstairs and he hears voices down there talking, and laughing.

Eric is dizzy, worn out, doesn't know what day it is. He smells his shirt; beer and bus fumes and *himself,* and the stronger sausage smell from downstairs reminds him that he hasn't eaten since his lunch break at the bus station in

Limerick. He doesn't remember what day that was, but he's ready for breakfast.

First, though, he takes a shower.

Downstairs, Mary sits with Phillip. He's finished his paper, and they have breakfast together. She passes him the teapot.

"His name's Eric?"

Phillip nods yes, pouring tea.

"Came in yesterday, a bit after you checked in. Lookin' a mess."

"I know. I saw him following me from the bus. Didn't worry me, though."

Phillip eats a tomato and nods again.

"Nor me. I thought he was a drunk at first. But he then just seemed tired. I've been tired like that, haven't you?"

Mary says yes.

"Of course, after that little show this morning maybe he's not *too* tired!"

Mary waves her hand in the air trying not to choke on her tea, finally swallows, and they can't stop laughing.

THE GREEN METAL CHAIR BY THE STREAM

KIERAN GETS UP EARLY, pats his wife's blanketed bottom in bed beside him, and pulls on his robe. He goes to the bedroom window, rubs his hands over the radiator, and looks out into the fog. Softly pulling the bedroom door closed he heads downstairs for the kitchen.

Along the way, he pauses at Chester's door and listens. He hears nothing and continues down the creaking stairs, still rubbing his hands to warmth.

Kieran will talk to anyone anytime about anything anywhere in Cork or on his spontaneous sudden trips out of town, but he gets up early every morning to be by himself.

And for this daily solitude, he has a routine and a route and a final destination, which is his friend out there in the fog —an old green metal chair. It sits rusting by the stream behind the hotel, strong enough to hold him.

The routine begins with his patting his wife's bottom in bed. Next, he goes to the window and radiator, then he goes downstairs to the kitchen. The routine wakes his wife every morning, but by the time he's in the kitchen, she's asleep again.

The night before, he has set this all up; his wide, squat, blue ceramic mug sits clean on the counter—a big, thick, heavy piece he made in an evening pottery class in Cork. He runs it under the cold early morning water in the sink. This is a favorite part of the routine. He rinses it and dries it on his thick towel of a robe. He makes tea and pours it in. He stands leaning against the kitchen counter, holding his mug in both hands. He looks out across the large kitchen and through the window to his chair in the backyard. *His chair.*

Every day, he wakes up this way, and he can't think of a better way to do it. He remembers how he used to do it. He had some of the same routine as now, but the final destination was a little TV set on the kitchen counter he'd sit in front of and stare at. He'd watch the cable news shows and morning celebrity updates, and he did this for a few years until he felt it weighing down on him one morning.

The morning he felt the most invaded and weighed down, Kieran took the TV set down to the basement and dropped it straight down hard in a corner on the concrete floor. He didn't even sweep up the broken screen glass. Heading back upstairs, he saw the old green metal chair and carried it up. He brought it out to the stream, looked around and up at the trees, then planted it firmly in the perfect spot.

He knew that day that he had changed his life. The change wouldn't be on TV, but he had done it.

Kieran walks to the back door of the kitchen, slips into a pair of worn-slick leather shoes. He has pulled the laces out of the shoes for the easy on and off, just a flick of the foot.

Kieran walks down the path to his chair. He has made a path with favorite stones, tree limbs, colorful leaves, and chunks of bark gathered from the side of the stream, and it's soft under his leather shoes. After he broke the TV that day, he'd spent the rest of the morning making the path.

He eases down onto the cold metal chair, cradles the thick hot mug in his hands, and closes his eyes. He remembers those mornings in the kitchen, hours going by, days going by, staring at the screen. It had made him and his life feel very little. On those mornings, the inn wasn't enough, or it was too far away from the world on TV, or Julie wasn't enough, or he thought he himself wasn't enough. Mainly, it was that last one.

He'd watch the cool confident up-to-date younger men in suits in the adverts in foreign airports and posh white hotel rooms and perfect beaches Facebooking and cell-phoning everywhere and everyone doing everything right and he'd wonder if he'd made a wrong turn somewhere to wind up here, working in an inn on the side of Cork.

Then, on this one particular morning, he kind of got sick of this way of thinking and he attacked the TV set.

It had been so easy to unplug the TV set, go downstairs and drop it shattering on the basement floor. The act had brought peace of mind instantly.

Of course, Julie bought a new TV a week later, but Kieran doesn't seem to notice.

There is only one way to be on TV, he'd come to understand back then. There is that one popular normal, on TV. But in the car and bus trips he had taken through all the little and big towns from Dingle to Farranfore to Kinsale to Ballyvourney to Cork, he'd seen a lot of *sort of* normals. And he'd seen some *not* so normals. And they'd all been friends of his for a drink or an afternoon, but one way or the other, friends for life, even if never seen again.

And as for Cork, well, there's nothing normal in Cork, he thinks this morning, watching the stream and sitting very still in his green metal chair.

Kieran is also thinking of the not normal one upstairs called Chester. He's up there now, hungover, probably almost broke, has a house but doesn't seem to have a job, seems lost and can't get back home, wherever that is.

Yes, that's how it is for him, the lucky bastard.

Kieran takes a long sip of tea.

I've been exactly that kind of lucky. Exactly where he needs to be.

WHEN, NOT IF ...

TODAY IS TOMMY'S DAY OFF and he's still in bed. He's lying there in bed humming some sort of song that he woke up with and he's thinking about Sondra's visit last night. He really remembers her lipstick and sunglasses on in the middle of the night and imagines her in this room, giving her "the tour" of this and then the other room. Lying there and looking up, he looks at the rust stains on the ceiling and thinks he'd better paint the place before she comes.

If that's to happen. Ok, when. Rob has been telling him to stop using the word if.

Tommy turns on the radio by the bed and hears a man singing, nearly screaming, and he hums along with him. He's up and singing with him, imagining Sondra watching him, and the woman next door knocks on the wall and Tommy stops. He tiptoes over to the window and there's Rob out on the street.

Rob is passing out sheets of paper to people on the street, flagging down cars and handing the papers into the car windows, waving them at trucks and buses, and sticking them into shop windows.

Most of these sheets wind up on the sidewalk, or fall down into the gutter. Rob seems absolutely unperturbed by this. He gathers up the sheets, moves down the street, and passes them out again.

The sheets say—

CORK HAS A NEW VOICE!
THE SONGBIRD HAS FLOWN
AND ITS NAME IS TOMMY LALLY!!!!

One sheet lands by Tommy's window and he says, "Oh, fuck's sake!"

THE FRESH SEA BREEZE OF HOPE

ROB WAS OUT OF BED at four this morning and started writing all these sheets out, one at a time. Towards dawn, he had begun to tire of it, especially making the exclamation marks, but he had stuck with it, and kept the exclamation marks after Tommy's name to *four* every time.

The paper he had stolen from his part-time, temp job in an office. He had a little stack of sealed packages of copy paper at home, stolen from the computer room at work. He had it in mind to be a poet or a songwriter, maybe even write movie scripts for Jim Sheridan, and so he would sneak off once in awhile with a package of fresh white empty pages. He had collected a stack of these packages of pages without opening or writing on any one of them just yet. But the packages sat in his apartment like a stack of unwritten books and he took great pleasure in sneaking a pack of paper out of his dull job, out of the office where nobody remembered his name. He'd sneak it out under his sweater and coat, wedged against his back down in his pants, and head to a pub. He'd order a pint at a table away from the bar, pull out the pack of paper and place it on the table. He'd look at the wrapped-up package of blank pages with great hope. "My collected works to be," he'd say to the pack of paper, and drink to himself, the future poet. He'd carry the package out of the pub like it was a book already published and for sale down the street at the bookstore.

And now he's broken open one of these packages and begun writing. Rob knows that these sheets aren't songs or poems or movies, but this is something he hasn't done before and he has gotten up at four a.m. to do it. It could lead to songs and poems ... or something.

So he's feeling good out in the street doing this, and he passes the sheets out until there are none left. Then, empty-handed and standing on the corner, he looks around at people stopping and reading his pages, he looks at the pages he's gotten into shop windows, and he watches as some of the pages flutter down the street. That's alright, he thinks; it'll fly down the street and lie there until someone picks it up and reads it. He's lit the fuse.

He's proud to see his work all over the street. He likes that his writing is in so many strangers' hands and in the middle of the shop windows. He feels he's dared something this morning.

Naturally, it's time to celebrate.

He decides Tommy is still asleep, so he looks around and walks back into the pub he's just hung a page in, and orders a pint.

Three pints later, Rob gets restless, pulls a pen from his coat, goes outside and picks up one of his stray pages from the sidewalk. He comes back inside to his table and, turning the page over to the blank side, holding the pen over the paper, ready to write, he begins to plan. The pen hangs over the paper. Rob looks over to the bar where a gang of men are standing, smiling at him. One of them waves him over, holding up a full pint glass. Rob smiles back and waves that he's coming, that he'll be right over. But first, he writes.

> There's so much to do. This is a new day.
> Indeed this is a new day.
> Don't know where to begin for Tommy,
> but I'll be his lucky man and his rock.
> I'll be his fresh sea breeze of hope.
> Today I begin.

Rob skips down and writes again. He's got all the rhyming words ready. It's been in his head all through the morning, this morning when he's felt as though he could do anything. It's a poem and he starts with the title.

FUCK MY JOB

All the dullness
All the drabness
Of the office
Will not suffice.
Completely hopeless,
I say
They can stick it
With sharpness
Up their orifice!

He holds the poem up and reads it. He turns his head sideways and frowns at it. He changes "orifice" to "orifices" and then back again to the one orifice. Then he experiments by putting in the word "arse" instead of orifice, but he doesn't hear it rhyming with anything except "sharpness," but just a little. He puts orifice back in. He kind of likes it and he kind of doesn't like it, but he folds the page up in a small square, sticks it in his pants pocket, and gets up from his table to join the men and drink with them.

"It's a new day," Rob says to himself on the way over.

... AND NOW, NOT LATER

A FEW BLOCKS AWAY and around the corner, Tommy studies his ceiling, wondering what color paint he should use to cover the rust stains up there.

He's humming. Then he's singing. The woman next door is knocking again. He keeps humming.

ANOTHER GREEN METAL CHAIR

KIERAN IS BACK in the kitchen again, and the dining room table is full of groggy but lit-up faces, shoulder to shoulder, the guests of the inn. Shoulder to shoulder strangers, having breakfast and talking like old friends. Laughing along with each other's conversation, but not too loudly. A large yellow chandelier glows down on the long wooden table, and the mixture of yellow and dark brown makes it warm and golden in the room.

Kieran has seen many kinds and combinations of people and he's experienced much more than his share of solitude, but this kind and pleasant thing that happens most mornings at his inn makes him happy.

He doesn't know how these people are out in the world, back out on the road, back in their homes and jobs. But here, on these mornings, they are unhurried and enjoying themselves and each other. Some of them have their hair neatly combed, some don't, nobody cares. The shyest guest is brought gently into conversation or just as thoughtfully left alone, without comment. And the loudest talker turns it down a bit, lets others in, and listens.

Kieran pours tea into his mug and stands in a corner of the kitchen, out of the lamp glow, and watches his guests. He thinks if he read in a travel book a description of what's happening in this room he'd laugh it off as sentimental advertising.

There had been the time, really most of his life, when he had laughed it off, even standing in the same room with it. Laughing at it, distrusting it, feeling apart from it, completely longing for it.

There's a skinny, bony face looking up at Kieran from the end of the table. It's lined with merry smiling wrinkles and has big blue eyes and white tousled hair. This man straightens up in his chair, looks at Kieran, and makes an announcement.

"My friends refer to me as Wee Willie of Wexford, but you seem a damn sight more Wee than ME! In years, I mean! I wouldn't want to be inferrin' a wee-ness in that OTHER department!"

Wee Willie laughs more at his own joke than anyone else, but when he slaps the table in front of him and knocks his teacup into his own lap, the rest of the table falls in with him, in laughter.

Kieran is quick and brings a towel to Wee Willie of Wexford, who is still laughing, but dancing a bit on his tip-toes with the heat of the hot tea spilled in his lap. The other guests are trying to help him clean up his mess but laughing too hard to be much help. And Wee Willie keeps on with his tip-toe dance going "Oh, oh, oh, JAYSUS! oh-oh-oh! It's HOT!"

Kieran goes over to the radio on the kitchen counter, which has been playing low soothing harp music. He turns the dial, finds a station playing a driving fiddle and whistle jig, and he turns it up loud. Wee Willie stops his dance a moment, listens with his blue eyes open wide, then starts dancing with the jig, the large damp stain all over his pants, and his hair flying wild in the air.

Pouring another mug of tea and then a cup of tea, Kieran takes these and goes upstairs. He goes to Chester's room and knocks on the door.

"Chester, I know you're not asleep in there, with all hell breaking loose down below!" The door opens and Chester is there in his red and green plaid boxer shorts and his grey herringbone cap on at an angle. He's laughing, too.

"What's going on in the dining room?" he asks, and takes the cup from Kieran.

"Wee Willie of Wexford, of course. And his *wee-willie* is a bit WET right about now! Come on, Chester, let's get breakfast. I want to talk to you."

He starts towards the stairs then notices Chester looking down at his boxer shorts and boots, hesitating. Kieran looks down there, too, and comes closer, chuckling.

"I don't think it matters, Chester. Wait'll you see the rest of them. You'll fit right in. Come as you are." And he walks on down the stairs, laughing and slapping his leg in time with the music on the radio.

Chester, in his underwear and cap, follows him down.

Later, with Wee Willie in dry pants and heading back to Wexford, Kieran sizzles blood sausages on the stove and brings bread to the table where he and Chester have set down plates and cups for breakfast.

"How long have you been in your house now, Chester?"

"A week."

"Do you like your house, Chester?" Kieran sits down and butters a thick chunk of the brown bread. He doesn't look directly at Chester as he asks these first questions.

"I do. It's still a bit empty, but I love it there already. Rob loaned me a sleeping bag and a pillow."

"How's the money holding out?" Kieran asks this and goes to a box on the kitchen counter and pulls out a short cigar. He looks in a drawer for matches and waits for the answer. There's a pause now, so he keeps looking for the matches he's got in his hand.

"Well, it's getting low, Kieran. But I'll make it. Tommy might have some kind of job at the pub, he said I could do some kind of temporary night clean up, maybe Friday and Saturday nights. He can't give me any full-time, but on those busy weekend nights he may have some work for me."

Kieran finally finds his matches and comes back to the table. He sits down and gets busy with the cutting of his stubby fat cigar, lighting it, and asks another question through the smoke.

"Rent due soon, eh?" He coughs and waves at the cigar smoke.

"Yes it is. Very soon. Yesterday." Chester has stopped eating.

"Well, now, that IS soon," says Kieran.

They both look down at the table and there's a silence between them. Chester wishes they'd left the radio on or that Wee Willie of Wexford would come dancing back in the door.

Instead, Kieran takes a long drink out of his big favorite mug and leans forward, arms on the table. He looks right at Chester under the yellow chandelier light and smiles at him, decided.

"Chester, I want you to keep that house. It suits you. And we'll throw that fuckin' slimy sleeping bag of Rob's in the River Lee, but what we have to do now is get some money flowing, and I guess what I'm doing now is offering you a job. And proud to." He looks Chester straight in the eye and belches. They both crack up laughing, and in the middle of the laughter, Chester asks Kieran what kind of job?

"Partner. You and me. Running this inn." Chester looks across the table at Kieran for some sign of this being a joke. Kieran looks right back at him, not blinking but smiling, and very serious.

Not knowing what else to do, Chester starts eating again. Kieran doesn't move.

Chester starts talking around a mouthful of food. "What about your wife? She's your partner, isn't she? I don't want to, I mean, surely she ..."

"Julie my partner? Oh like hell, she is! She's no partner! Fuck sake, no, lad, she's in *charge!* She had this place long before I knew her, when I was on the road and wasn't a partner to a piece of shite! Oh no, she's had this place twenty years and I've been here for, well I don't know how long I've been here, that's all beside the point. But she complains these days, kind of out of the blue, and more and more so lately, that we don't get away on holiday anymore. We used to go on car trips to Dingle all the time, the Aran Islands, at least as far as Kinsale. We missed a party up in Temple Bar last Christmas because it's just the two of us here. She says we're not having enough fun nowadays. Sad, ain't it?"

And now, another silence between them.

Kieran puffs slowly on the cigar and watches Chester's face. He leans back in his chair, back out of the yellow lamp light, and blows cigar smoke in the air. From back there in the dim light and smoke he asks another question.

"You're on a weekly rent, then?"

"Yes," Chester says.

The legs of Kieran's chair hit the floor and he's up again. He walks over to a cupboard and pulls down another wooden cigar box. He starts counting out money from the box. Chester gets up from the table and walks over to the window. He looks out at the backyard and the stream. He sees a green metal chair.

Chester feels Kieran walking heavily on the old wooden kitchen floor towards him. And then he feels an arm go around his shoulders. Kieran hands Chester an envelope that has "Paycheck #1" written on it. They stand there like that, looking out at the backyard.

"Guess I'll have to get another chair," says Kieran.

They stand another moment looking out the window, then Kieran turns to Chester.

"Is it a deal then, lad?"

"Yes, it is, Kieran. It's a deal."

They stand back from each other and shake hands.

Suddenly, and before this moment becomes awkward, Kieran thinks of something and darts over to the basement door.

"I just thought of it, I happen to have a good spare bed down there somewhere for your house," he says, going down the stairs. "And you can damn well set fire to that slimy mat Rob gave you, bless his soul just the same."

Chester hears him thumping down the stairs and after a bit of silence, he hears him laughing. There's the sound of tinkling glass.

"Oh, and I have a grand TV set for you as well!"

ONE MEETING AFTER ANOTHER

JULIE STANDS BAREFOOT in the grass in front of the inn and wiggles her toes in the dew. She holds a clay mug of mail-order tea from India and looks out on the empty foggy morning road.

She hears her husband and Chester talking inside the inn. They're having the first official business meeting of the new partnership. Since she's the owner, Julie listens in.

"Well, Chester, can you cook?"

"Yes."

"Can you make beds and clean the rooms?"

"Yes."

"You'll have to take reservations and greet the guests sometimes."

"Right."

"Julie mostly handles the books and the money, but we'll need you to shop for food every once in awhile ... eggs, sausages, vegetables, coffee, milk, tea, soap, whiskey ... all that stuff."

"Can do."

"Right. So how about Monday and Tuesday off and you take the weekends for awhile so me and the woman can sleep in or take off and have fun? Or take off, have fun and sleep in, if you know what I mean."

"I'm your man."

"Meeting adjourned. Let's have a drink."

Julie checks her watch. She has forty-five minutes until *her* meeting down in Cork. She can still taste last night's wine on her tongue, even as she drinks the tea. She hopes the tea will cover the wine smell on her breath when she's at the meeting. She knows she'd better get clothes on if she's going to make the meeting on time, so she goes upstairs and gets dressed in old faded almost-white blue jeans and a tight black sweater. She slides her feet into paint-spattered leather clogs, goes downstairs, gets into the shuttle van, and drives towards Cork.

That wine taste on her tongue. Like a trigger. Like a song or a smell, a drink of wine or gin or stout becomes a memory reaching back through the past in this town, reaching back to good or bad mornings or long afternoons or evenings, or any number of Christmas's or one-night or one-weekend stands. And Julie wonders if she can do without that trigger.

Drinking, for her, has always been so *sentimental.*

She wonders if everyone in Cork has to drink all day to feel ok. She wonders if she'll always have to. She's starting to think that the fun is going out of it. Still makes her feel sentimental though. The good old days, the good old days, all that stuff. These days, nowadays, she's thinking, seem to be getting so flat, without some kind of something extra.

Though she loves her life with Kieran, she looks back a lot lately, and now, as she drives towards town, she's looking back again.

She remembers her first flat in Cork and her job at the newspaper as an obituary writer. *That* was interesting, talking to funeral homes and weeping families every night. There was a kind of dress code there in the newspaper city room, and she ignored it, colorfully.

She had a long, one-room warehouse flat on the top floor and it was empty except for the two corners. Her bedroom corner and her living room corner, where she had guests. She had guests in the bedroom corner too.

She had three dresses back then, a black one, a red one, and a green one, all velvet and short. And on the brick wall near the window, there were three ten-penny nails pounded in by whoever lived there before, so she hung her three dresses on those three nails. She had a pair of long black leather boots that zipped up above her knees. At night she would stand them up under the three dresses. Also a small stack of black woolen sweaters, which, she thought, made her breasts look big.

Julie drives into a parking space under her old top-floor apartment. She looks up at the window. She used to sit in this window at night, looking out across Cork, and out beyond it to the horizon line of lights on the hill, wondering about life beyond the town. She'd had Dublin dreams and London dreams and she could almost see them through this window. The dreams were sort of unclear but always had to do with more people around, more fun, music, falling in love with somebody, and then something to do with Art.

She was never quite sure about that last one, about what the art dream was going to be, she just didn't want to be in a normal job and life. Anything but that. Anything. Her father had been like that. Dreaming, looking out of all of his windows as well.

Julie looks up at the window and thinks how brave that was of her, more than twenty years ago, to absolutely decide against that usual kind of life. Whatever comes, she had said then, I'll just be poor and do what I want and that's that. In the days when she had made this big decision, she was in her mid-twenties, sleeping with many men, listening to music in her flat, hearing it and dancing to it in the clubs, making paintings on the wall of her flat, making paintings right there on the wall, writing long, long stretches of sentences in art sketchbooks, filling up many pages, some nights sitting by that window in a chair, and waiting for the phone to ring. Or for something to occur to her, some inspiration from somewhere. And she'd drink and dream. And drink.

As Julie sits in the van underneath her old window she realizes and laughs at what she was like in that time, before cell phones and answering machines and all the rest of it, when she would wait for hours for a guy to call her, and if he still hadn't by midnight, she'd take the phone, on its long extension cord, into her bedroom and sit it right down by her head as she went to sleep. By that time she was drunk and her ears ringing from standing by the tall stereo speakers with all the lights out, but she would hear that phone when it rang. If it did.

And for Julie, sitting in the van under this window with all its memories, none of this feels like twenty-three years ago at all, even with all the technological talking advances. That thing of sitting in the window at night waiting for something, she still feels something like that now. She sits in her car, staring up at the window and she realizes she's doing it again, but instead of staring out of the window, waiting, she's staring up at the window, from the other side, still waiting.

She breaks off staring up at the window and looks down at the instrument panel of the Kieran's Inn Shuttle Van. She's amazed somehow by all of these dials, some of which she's mystified by. Julie never had any kind of car when she lived on this street. She had the monthly laminated bus pass but mostly she walked and walked and walked.

She hears a door opening and laughter to her left, from the apartment building.

A young couple is coming out the door, struggling with a baby stroller. The woman has long shiny black hair and beams at the baby while the man lifts the pram through the door and sets it down on the front walk. He is very strong and fit in his clean white sweater and new khaki pants, and the woman holds onto him by his strong arm as they walk down the street. They both carry many little black devices and check them as often as they check the baby, more often really.

Julie puts on her sunglasses and watches the little family walk down the street, then she pops open her glove box and pulls out a worn leather pouch. She has three joints rolled inside and she pulls the fattest one out and lights it, sliding down a bit more in her seat. She looks up again at the window and remembers getting high up there, looking out at the night horizon.

She watches the little family move happily down the street. She can't figure out how the buildings and the street are all the same, twenty-three years later. The couple has different clothes and hairstyles and the pram is not a cheap silver aluminum thing rolling along on little rubber wheels but a large black plastic modern almost car. Still, everything else seems the same to Julie.

She sits in the van, holding in long drags of marijuana smoke, watching the family disappear around the corner. She is feeling a bit more contented now, watching yellow autumn leaves blow across the street. Some things are the same, she knows. She watches the leaves blow and she remembers walking all around this neighborhood. She looks up one more time at the window of her old flat and gives it a little wave, and catches herself in the rear-view mirror, smiling. She starts the van and pulls out very slowly. Drives very carefully and slowly, the marijuana working on her.

Now she worries that maybe someone will smell that on her at the meeting.

The street curves along like a half-moon, curving to the left, and she sees the little young family again, coming to a small line of new stores and restaurants. There are other young people inside these shops, and sitting outside, very leisurely, at tables. Julie pulls over again behind a big jeep sort of *truck* kind of car, really huge on the little street, and when she shuts off the van and it backfires like a gun, she slides down again. It's getting busier on the street with more couples and students walking past.

Julie watches. The one place they all seem to be going is the Starbucks on the corner. They all have the same white cups with the same brown cup holders and they all go in there and relax in the same way, she thinks. Julie feels less and less relaxed, sliding even lower in her seat.

She looks at the clock on the instrument panel. The meeting is in fifteen minutes.

She takes a long, last, deep drag on her joint and straightens up in her seat, taking off her shades, tossing them on the dashboard. In the rear-view mirror, she's smiling like the devil.

"Fuck 'em," she says out loud. "I used to live here." She starts the engine again, turns on the radio, and rolls down the window. She puts in her CD of *The Pretenders* and turns it up.

The same music from twenty-three years ago.

She pulls out nice and slow and purrs the van along slowly, her left hand beating out the rhythm of the song on the driver's side door. She hopes she's disturbing the leisure of the Starbucks scene on the sidewalk. They've been watching her since the backfire. The little family from her old building stares at her, even the baby in the pram stares at her, with pretty much the same expression as her parents.

She brings the joint to her lips and takes a long drag in front of everyone on the sidewalk, smiles, and drives along slowly.

Julie drives down the street away from the stores. None of these places were here twenty-three years ago, she thinks, especially not Starbucks. There was, then, one huge old renovated warehouse turned into a waterbed and water pipe store called *The Buddha Slug*. She had bought a great deal of what she is now smoking out of the back room of *The Buddha Slug*, now out of business.

With five minutes to go until the meeting, Julie pulls into an empty church parking lot. She thinks of firing up a second joint and driving back to the inn. But lights are on inside a room in the church, and there's someone carrying a tall stack of styrofoam cups past a window. She's puzzled, though, with no cars in the lot or on the street. She tamps out her joint in the ashtray, waves a hand around to clear the air, and cracks the window down an inch. She takes a deep breath and gets out of the van, walks through the back door of the church, and makes a right turn down the hallway towards the room.

There's a long table and an old stained silver coffee machine on a counter in the otherwise bare room. A young orange-haired guy stands by it, staring at it. He looks up at Julie very suddenly and tries to smile.

"Hello how are you do you know how to work this thing?" he says very fast, walking over with one hand out to shake. Julie takes his hand and shakes it, feeling how wet and trembling it is.

"Just us two so far," he says, again very fast, and walks back to the coffee machine. Julie walks over and opens cabinets until she finds a can of coffee. Eric takes the lid and the filter off the machine and they begin to make the coffee together. It takes awhile, but after shaking hands with him, Julie no longer worries about smelling like pot.

After awhile more, the old coffee machine wheezes to a stop, puffs out steam, and they each pour a cup of coffee. Julie stirs milk in with a wooden stick and looks at the clock on the wall. They sit down at a long table next to each other.

Julie thinks how, in all those years of living right around the corner, walking through the snow at night, sweating in the long afternoon summer heat of this neighborhood, and buying marijuana from *The Buddha Slug* next door, she has never been inside this church before. It had always been here, she'd even had sex in the grass behind this church one summer night, her and some passionate young clumsy wonder who looked just like this young guy sitting at the table with her.

It's just the two of them, listening to the whirring of the electric clock on the wall. Eric looks at the clock, it's five minutes past the meeting time. He looks at Julie, smiles, and clears his throat.

"Hi, I'm Eric. I'm an alcoholic," he says.

"Hello, Eric. I'm Julie. I'm an alcoholic," she says.

They don't seem to know what to do next, and there's no one else around, so now it's just the sound of the whirring clock on the wall again. Julie takes a sip from her cup and starts to choke.

"This coffee is shit, isn't it, Eric?"

He starts laughing and spits the coffee on his shirt.

"Yes, Julie, shit would be the word for it!"

LADDY LUCK

ROB GOES TO TOMMY'S DOOR and knocks, a very big smile on his face. He has plans, plans, plans for Tommy's singing career; nothing you could really write down yet, nothing very specific in that way, but the ideas and dreams in Rob's head are vast and grand and unbounded.

Rob knocks again, and sings to the door, "Oh Tommy boy, Oh Tommy boy, oh, it's a new day and Laddy Luck is shining on you, well, Jesus, he's here and knockin' on your door!" Still nothing and silence, so Rob tries the door. It's locked. He waits a moment longer, then shrugs and turns back to the sidewalk.

"I'll find ya, Tommy," says Rob, still smiling, walking down the street. "Things aren't so normal lately around here," he thinks. Then aloud, he says, "Just a feeling. Just something new."

And he turns left at the next corner where he usually turns right.

SING

TOMMY SITS IN THE DARK upstairs balcony of the University College Theater watching music students singing below. He has snuck upstairs to the balcony and watches the students do their warm-up exercises and loosening-up exercises, shaking their arms loose and massaging each other. There's lots of laughter and joking between the students, and Tommy feels so much older than them. The fun they're having with each other, and the confidence they seem to have with their singing makes the balcony feel much higher away from the stage and lonelier for Tommy, but then he shakes his head and straightens up in his chair.

"Don't start with that again, Tommy," he whispers to himself. "Don't be thinking that way again. You've come here to learn something. Today the balcony, tomorrow the stage, I say! Or the next day," he allows, with a smile.

He has said all this in a low whisper to himself, but there are a couple of the students looking up towards where he is. He slides back into the dark, down low in his balcony chair, trying to hold back laughter. The students look up towards him, then at each other, then back up again, but a teacher has arrived on the stage so their attention is back downstairs again. Tommy makes a choking sound in his throat, trying to hold back laughing, and now all the students look up at the balcony. The teacher, trying to start the class, sees where they're looking and looks that way too. Tommy slides even lower in his chair, practically on the floor now and shaking with silent laughter. He's not sure *why* he's hiding, but keeps sliding down onto the floor.

"Is there someone there?" The teacher, hands on hips, has turned towards where Tommy is. He walks over to the piano on the stage and puts on glasses and again asks, "Well?"

Tommy is on the floor hidden and wondering why he is hiding. He sticks a hand up and that's what the students and the teacher see from below, just a hand deep in the balcony, held up in surrender.

Tommy stands up slowly, straightens his jacket, and brushes off his pants. "Hello," he says. He seems to be tipping a hat he doesn't have, to be polite.

"Can we help you please?" The teacher asks this in a low perfectly articulated theatrical voice. The students hear it and smile at his way of taking over a room, taking over a situation, taking over a person. They nod at each other and smile, letting each other know that each of them knows the importance of the man, their teacher, even though he's been yelling at them, in a perfectly articulated way, for a whole semester now, making fun of them when they sing in this, a singing class, but they recognize his genius and know that any yelling he does at them is for their own good.

Though each of their voices gets more and more strangled when they come to the theater.

But they know that they'll grow from the experience of being around what he calls his "artistic honesty." This is not at all questioned. "It will be good for me, even while he's yelling and belittling me," the thinking of the student group goes, so nobody quits the class. Because the thinking goes, as the teacher has told them, "I will take each of you to the next level."

Meanwhile, on the next level, Tommy goes up the stairs to get out of the balcony.

"No no no, please don't leave." This catches Tommy at the top of the stairs. He turns around slowly and looks back down to the stage. The teacher, the students standing behind him, are all looking up at him. The teacher is smiling.

"Can we help you?"

Tommy says *fuck* to himself up there in the dark and walks down a few stairs.

"I'm a singer, or trying to be, and I thought I'd maybe watch the professionals to get some um, tips or something, see how it's done, you know?" Tommy says fuck again, but they can't hear him. The teacher takes his glasses off and twirls them in one hand as he walks across the stage, thinking. The students are beginning to laugh a little, gathering in a bunch in the middle of the stage. The teacher has apparently stopped thinking because he's put the glasses back on and stopped walking.

"A singer or trying to be. I see. Have you performed here in Cork? What was your name?" The teacher is at the lip of the stage, a spotlight flashing off his glasses.

"The name's John, sir, and I have done some singing in Shane's Pub, which is where I work," Tommy says, and he can really feel those eyes of the teacher burning into him though he can't see them.

"Done some singing in—what was it—Shane's Pub?Which is where you work. OK, I think I've got it." He turns upstage to the students. "People—this is John from Shane's Pub!" More laughter from the students, some of them carrying on with stretching exercises, some of them half-waving up at "John."

"Um, John, could you come downstairs, I'm having trouble seeing you."

Tommy walks to the exit out of the balcony, and on the way downstairs passes the exit out of the theater, and almost goes that way. Instead, he continues down to the first floor and up towards the front of the stage. When he gets there he stops in the front row of seats and the teacher looks down at him.

"You know, um—*John*—we're certainly glad that you've come, but if you'd like to audit this class, and that's also fine, there's a small matter of actually enrolling, and that's fine, that's fine, but um, the thing is ... these students have come through many years of training and paid their way here, so really, what I think I'd like to ask of you now is to simply ... sing. Give us a song, eh?"

Tommy looks past the teacher at the students who are looking down at the stage.

"Oh, I know you haven't the benefit of your mates at Shane's Pub or your, well, I have no idea as to whether you've had anything to drink yet or not, so we'll let that go. But could you maybe give us something right now, something, well, what should it be? Say ... 'Danny Boy?' Could you do that for us right now, John?"

And the teacher walks over to a folding chair and sits down. Waiting.

Many things go through Tommy's mind in a flash, and in the silence and stillness of the theater he feels his whole life go by. He thinks of other teachers he's had. He thinks of other insults he's had. He remembers the night on the Irish Sea. He thinks of Rob and Chester and he remembers last night singing by himself and then Sondra coming in and kissing him and this brings him courage, it cuts through the silence, though in this silence he can't imagine being able to open his mouth to speak, let alone sing.

And he woke up today feeling so free and brave.

The large empty silent university theater terrifies him. The teacher sitting and staring at him terrifies him. The sympathetic-looking students embarrass him. But before he has thought about doing it he takes off his jacket and drapes it over a front-row seat. He looks at the teacher and forces himself to lift his chin. He takes his hands out of his pockets and forces his arms to hang down and at least *look* relaxed. He looks over at the students, back at the teacher. Then he finds a stained spot on the stage curtain and looks at that.

He takes a deep breath and knows that once he's inhaled as much as he can he will have to start singing and that's the end of his thinking about anything and then he's already into the first line of the song.

CLICKING AND JINGLING

SONDRA AND NEPO come clicking (her high heels) and jingling (his leash) happily down South City Link Road through the wild windblown crowds of shoppers and workers. The shoppers and workers are moving fast in the cold with either hats on or hair blowing wild, and all of them with little clouds of steam coming out of their mouths. The wind blows down into the street from the blue sky where the clouds are racing each other across the tops of the Cork buildings.

She and Nepo are feeling good and taking big strides along the sidewalk, Sondra by feet, Nepo by inches, but big inches!

Sondra is taking a lunch break from the shelter with Nepo to find him some new little stuffed animal toys and a big bag of shelter food for the week. She will then buy herself the three presents she's planned on since last payday—the sharp tailored green corduroy jacket with pockets and gold buttons and padded shoulders in the window of a new store full of French clothes; then, in the same store, a new lacy bright red brassiere (also French); and then, at last, a bottle of French champagne.

She likes the bottle because of the beautiful label which looks like a Van Gogh painting. This too, she has only seen in the window of the wine store. She hasn't tasted the champagne, doesn't know a thing about it, but will buy it and won't ask for the advice of the wine store man. She will buy it mostly because of the label which completely fits in with her style. Which is French, these days. Everything French. Sondra is in a French stage.

Nepo and Sondra come to the door of Tommy's bar, where they had been very early this morning. Sondra runs a hand through her hair, straightens her sunglasses, and peeps in the window while Nepo pees on the door. She means to pop her head in and say hello to Tommy again, and also to see if he's singing, right in the middle of the day, with people around this time!

But Tommy is not here, the pub is dark, there are three old men at the bar and the only sound in the room is not music or singing but soccer on the television screen.

Sondra looks down at Nepo looking up at her. He blinks the little hairs around his eyes and looks down the street, not wagging his tail.

"Come on then, Nepo," she says. "We'll see him sometime." And they walk down the street.

She was hoping to hear him singing again. She worried a little about coming back so soon, but she wanted to see him again this morning.

She wonders where he is and if he's singing.

AND KEEP SINGING

TOMMY HAS FINISHED singing "Danny Boy." The theater is absolutely silent. There's a chill in the air and his whole body is tingling. He is shaking but not for the same reason he was a few minutes ago.

The teacher has his hand up and his head down. The students are standing still on the stage, not sitting or leaving or moving or stretching or doing anything. The teacher drops his hand and says something softly to himself, looking down and away from Tommy, who is smiling from ear to ear.

"Um, John, would you please come up here?" He looks down at Tommy, who's still smiling broadly. Tommy points at the stage and shrugs. The teacher nods and waves him up.

"Yes, John, here, up here. Come." The teacher stands up and walks to the back of the stage rubbing his forehead and sighing. The students stand still. The only sound is Tommy walking up the steps and onto the stage. The teacher turns around.

"Alright John, come over here to me." The teacher motions Tommy closer with his fingers, not looking at him. And Tommy goes. He walks to the teacher's hand until the fingers become a fist telling him to stop. The teacher takes a deep breath and finally looks at Tommy.

He looks long at Tommy. He looks at Tommy's shoes and pants and shirt and finally, he looks at his head. That's how Tommy feels, that it's his head that's being looked at more than his face.

"BREATHE, John, BREATHE!" The teacher demonstrates by breathing himself, long and deep, and holding his breath, eyes closed. There is a long silence. Tommy watches. The teacher exhales at last through pursed lips, eyes still closed. He opens his eyes and refocuses on Tommy, who backs up a step.

And to Tommy he says, "Will you do this please?" He is pleading with Tommy. The students stand still on the stage.

Tommy takes in a deep breath and he's going to give it a good brave try. The teacher lunges at Tommy.

"No, no, no, no, NO! I said BREATHE! BREATHE!" The teacher has his hands on Tommy's stomach and he's pushing. Tommy loses his breath and is coughing, choking, kind of laughing, and he can't stop smiling.

The teacher pushes hard on Tommy's gut, his other hand on his chest, his face close to Tommy's head. "BREATHE!"

Again, Tommy takes in a breath, as deep as he can take it, still feeling he's doing something wrong. The teacher's eyes are closed again.

"Make a sound, John," he whispers, opening his eyes and leaning in close to Tommy. "DON'T think, make a sound, GO!"

Tommy starts in on the song again. "Oh Danny BOY..."

"NO! No, no, no, no, make a SOUND! And let it come up from down here, let it be organic!" begs the teacher, and squeezes a roll of Tommy's big belly. And he whispers close to Tommy, "Be an animal! You are a BEAST! Don't think, don't think, don't think now Tommy—BREATHE and ..."

And Tommy yells as loud as he can.

The teacher lets go of Tommy and walks off to the side of the stage by himself.

"Ok, John, ok. Well, you are an animal. You are a particular sort of animal, a recognizable one clearly, but as far as a singer, well, that's certainly in question." The teacher says this, walks over to Tommy, reaches up and ruffles Tommy's hair like he's a shamed small boy instead of a large man, getting larger by the moment, and still for some reason smiling.

"John, you come in here with all your yearning and your passion and your version of 'Danny Boy' and your dreams of singing, but what I heard when you sang was merely a sort of BELLOWING. Just a bellowing. And I've interrupted our class for you because I thought I saw something. I like to think of myself as someone who would do that, who would be open to that. Who knows talent. But I'm often wrong and just as often disappointed." He lets go with a very long sigh which seems to nearly completely deflate and collapse him on the stage, and repeats, "... often wrong and just as often ..." But he can't finish it.

The teacher walks over to his students and stands with them, his head down again, looking at the floor of the stage. A young blonde singer puts her hand on his shoulder. A student on the other side of the teacher does the same and looks down at the floor in a show of sympathetic unison and the rest of them just look and look and look at Tommy, poor fellow. The teacher looks now at Tommy too, with great sympathy showing, though he does notice the big unaccountable smile on Tommy's face.

"Tell me, John, do you really know what the song 'Danny Boy' is about at all? Or is it merely a pub song you sing at last call when you and everyone else are too drunk to notice that you cannot actually sing? You can't just want to do something and then it happens. Like I always say, *Passion without panache presents problems.*"

Now Tommy looks down at the stage. Trying not to laugh.

"John, I think maybe you might be able to sing, in time, with the proper years of training, but really John, I sense a real lack. Do you really think that the way that you sang carried any emotion? Were you IN the song? Were we feeling anything? I don't think that you were really there, really present. I really don't, John. There was no emotion."

The teacher leans forward from the waist at an almost right angle to himself to painfully make one final point.

"There were absolutely no colors whatsoever."

And still the unaccountable smile on Tommy.

The teacher creeps forward in his crouched-over, right angle position, towards Tommy, but stops and straightens up. All of the sympathy falling out of his face.

"You can't sing," he says. "I'm simply being honest with you. I just don't want you to be deluded about this and only get hurt later." The students standing with him nod *yes, that's true, you can't sing John*, but Tommy is looking out into the theater, shaking his head, amazed at something he's finally figured out.

"Sir, that's not what I came here to know. It turns out that's not what I came here for at all. And I am sorry to have taken up so much time. All of you, I'm sorry for that. That was rude of me. Kind of crazy, I guess. Still, I ... oh, never mind, anyway I'll be on my way now." Tommy walks off the stage, down the stairs, and he's humming. He stops and turns back. "Again, sorry for the trouble, but I would like to thank you. Thank you."

And as he walks up the aisle he's shaking his head again and humming.

The teacher walks to the edge of the stage and shades his eyes from the lights, trying to find Tommy in the dark.

"So John, are you saying that you don't care about honesty? I was being truthful with you. Do you not care about that?"

Tommy is in the dark but they can hear that his humming has turned to singing because he's back into "Danny Boy." And then the singing turns to laughter.

"No sir, I don't care about that. And the name is Tommy, by the way. Just being honest, you know."

This is Tommy turning.

A LITTLE SURPRISE AT THE END

AFTER THE INTERVIEW, Mary comes back upstairs and goes inside her dark room, the sunlight glowing green through the heavy patterned drapes, and she shuts the door behind her.

She leans against the door and exhales into the silent room. She can hear the workmen outside her window, in the alley below, loading things into trucks and laughing. She stares into the dark green light of the room and shakes her head.

Mary sits down on the edge of her bed and holds up her room key. She's astounded by how short the interview was. It had started in the usual awkward way, with the usual kinds of things like "Tell me about yourself" and then another question, something about her hobbies or something, and then "Why should I hire you?" and more like that. On and on.

And then something else happened.

Something else happened and the light and the feeling in the manager's office had changed and so had the look in his eyes. And Mary felt something very, very different as well. It happened in a moment, in a sentence. She could not have planned it. She didn't know she was going to say it or even remember it.

First though, the questions.

Phillip, retiring manager and owner of the Rose Lodge, asked Mary why she wanted to move to Cork from Kinsale, why she wanted to change things at this late stage of her life, and what was she looking for here? He asked these routinely, and smiling, but like he'd asked it dozens of times before, by habit, and hadn't ever wanted to, and really not wanted to with this sweet little old lady. He wasn't looking at her when it was her turn to answer these questions, but he kept smiling.

He had the handwritten resume on his desk that listed her managing a teashop in Kinsale as her life's work.

Mary answered the questions, though Phillip felt she answered them with sentences that were not really *her* sentences. She was just trying to get through this interview, same as he was. He could sense that she wasn't looking at him when she answered his questions, just as he wasn't looking at her.

But her voice was getting more and more shaky and soft, which he thought was unusual for a job interview, so Phillip kept the interview going longer than usual. He looked over at her when he thought she wasn't looking. And then he'd ask some new and equally dull question, even as he was trying to think of a better one. He didn't really know what to do with her.

There was, on the wall to the side of his large beat-up wooden desk, a wooden shelf, handmade by him, and on it a collection of dainty teacups. He walked over to this shelf as he waited for what he thought would be a dull answer to his last dull question. He took down a beautiful green cup with a scalloped edge and a matching saucer. He placed it in front of her, on top of her resume.

The room was so quiet in the moment that he set the teacup down on her resume Mary thought the interview was over. He poured the tea.

Her mind was wandering out of the room, out of the lodge, and back to the return bus to Kinsale, but Mary asked him to repeat his last question.

Phillip walked across the creaky wooden floor and back around his desk, pouring tea into his cup, and dropped down heavily into his chair.

"Mary, what would you bring to our little Rose Lodge?"

He looked at her, hating his rote interview question, smiling but wanting to get this over with.

Mary said, *"And in the end, the love you take is equal to the love you make."*

By some synchronized miracle of uncomfortable and sweet awkwardness, they both took a sip of tea at the exact same moment.

Mary, frowning then smiling and shaking her head, looked surprised and puzzled by what she'd just said. Phillip was smiling a little differently now too, and he tilted back in his red leather swivel chair swiveling his shoes up onto his desk.

The room was quiet again, and that quiet felt a little different to them now as well. Phillip looked over at Mary with new eyes.

"Abbey Road, right?"

"Last song."

"Last line?"

"Except for that bit about getting a belly full of wine."

"Oh, right, right. That little surprise at the end."

Then they were quiet and sat listening to last night's guests checking out in the lobby, loading the trunk of their car in the front lot. They sat for awhile like that, looking out the window, each holding their teacups and thinking about the Beatles.

Phillip swiveled his feet off his desk and stood up.

"I would be quite pleased to be replaced by *you* as the new manager of the Rose Lodge, Mary."

And now, back upstairs in her room, Mary hums the Beatles song and opens the windows wide, letting in a strong cold wind. She hears cars and conversation and Cork City outside her window and wants to get out there and walk. She looks for her walking shoes and starts to change into them but stops, and digs into her suitcase for something.

She finds the something, a paperback book, thick and new and still in its bookshop bag. She takes it out of the bag and looks at the title—*Taking Charge of the Job Interview and GETTING THAT DREAM JOB!*

Still humming, Mary walks over to the window again. She takes the book by its spine and flings it sideways out the window. The book hits the back wall of the dumpster below with a loud PONG and drops into the trash.

One of the workmen looks up and says, "Good one, Mum!"

ERIC, REST IN PEACE

IT'S BEEN A LONG COLD WINDY DAY in Cork and the sun is almost down. The water ripples freezing cold dark blue on the River Lee and the lights are coming on in the restaurants.

It's time to go to dinner for the couples walking along the river and it's time to go to work for some of the ones getting off the buses or walking alone, already looking tired.

Eric has been walking around Cork all day, walks along the river and is already drunk, though he was at that meeting today about not being drunk. Well, *one of these days*, he thinks, looking out over the glittering river. He remembers the woman he'd met this morning in the meeting, Julie. He liked her, he was glad she'd been there. She'd been fifty percent of the meeting, him being the other fifty.

He thinks maybe one more bar, and once he gets there he'll order another beer and write down some of these things he's been thinking about all afternoon. He can write down his plans for what he's going to do in Cork now that he's here. He's not going back to Limerick, he knows that for certain.

It's getting colder and Eric figures he had better at least figure out what he's going to do right now. He gives up on the bar idea, and he can't remember now what it was he was going to write down though it was just a second ago. He's swaying badly, with his back against the iron rail by the riverside.

Suddenly, there's a loud chiming of bells behind him. He turns around and there's a church tower on the far riverbank. Looking up high, he focuses on the round yellow clock face and the bells finish banging out six.

"It's going to be a long night," he says to himself. He holds onto the rail to steady himself but his hands begin to shake as much as the rest of his body.

He looks up at the church tower a little longer, thinking how pretty it is. The yellow illuminated clock face in the stone church tower with dark blue sky behind it. Lower in the sky it's a lighter blue with the sun just dropping below the horizon.

He looks back up at the clock face but it's starting to skitter and jump sideways, so he stops looking at it.

"It's going to be a long night," he says again. It's been a long day, too. He remembers the woman at the meeting in the church this morning, they talked about drinking, about drinking too much, and she was nice to him. Then he remembers he has a room in some inn somewhere and a painting he liked in the hall outside his room and he thinks he had better get back there now but he can't remember where it is. And then he remembers being naked out in the hallway with the woman from the bus standing there.

Eric looks at the church tower again, and now there's no blue on the horizon line, there's no horizon line at all, and he can't focus on the clock face anymore. He buttons up his jacket, sees a liquor store down the street, and walks in that direction.

Eric carries his bag of beer towards the church. As he crosses a bridge, he looks up trying to find the clock face again, but he doesn't see it. He can't see the faces of the other people passing him on the bridge but he hears their laughter and talking and shoes clicking on the walk. He smells their cigarettes.

Eric walks across the bridge as fast as he can without staggering and then he is off the bridge and walking in grass. He doesn't hear voices anymore, he's alone. He stops in the grass and sets down the bag of beer, takes a bottle out. He looks up to where he thinks the clock is and finds it, but it's still moving sideways in his eyes.

Eric is surrounded by gravestones. He sits down on one of them and pops open the bottle of beer with a little tin opener he carries. The beer foams up out of the bottle and down the side. Eric spreads his legs to avoid the spill, and the beer drips down onto the gravestone he's sitting on. It stains down across the face of the gravestone and seeps into the engraved letters of the dead.

Eric watches this for a long moment, and begins shaking and laughing, tears in his eyes. He takes a long drink from the bottle. He looks up at the bridge and watches people walking across the river into Cork.

He looks down into his bag. There are five bottles of beer for the night.

"What am I doing out here?" Eric says out loud. He looks around the cemetery for somewhere to sleep. He knows now that he can't make the bridge, let alone find the inn, let alone get up the stairs to his room without seeing anyone in the hall. And though he's really cold, he decides he'll drink all five beers and sleep here somewhere, in the cemetery.

It's some comfort to him knowing that this is where he'll sleep tonight, that he doesn't have to make that long trip back to his room. Somewhere in this graveyard he'll find a place to lie down and rest tonight, but for now, he drinks the beer.

Eric gets off the gravestone and sits on the ground, leaning against the stone. He reads the engraved name, lifts his bottle and says, "Rest well, Flynn, rest well!" He drinks the bottle of beer and stretches his legs out along the same lines he figures Flynn's legs are laid.

He takes off his glasses, folds them and slips them carefully into his inside jacket pocket.

"Can't see nothin' anyway, Flynn," he says. He drinks and steadies the bottle between his legs. He leans forward and digs his hands into the earth above Flynn and brings them together and rubs the grass and soil into his palms. He brings a hand to his face and smells it.

"Is this what you're smellin' then, Flynn?"

Eric rests his head on the gravestone. He looks up at the blurry yellow shape of the clock face. He can't see the clock hands, but he knows what time it is. It's time to piss. So he rolls over onto his knees and stands up, leaning on Flynn's gravestone. Still leaning, he unzips his pants with his other hand and lets go, pissing into the grass.

Eric doesn't zip his pants back up and starts digging in his jacket for his glasses. He finds them and tries to put them on but drops them. He bends down to find them in the darkness but grabs the glasses too hard and knocks a lens out. He puts them on and starts laughing again, squinting one eye in the empty frame, looking around with the other eye for the lens, somewhere on the ground, and the bag of beer.

He finds the bag of beer by the sound of rustling paper and starts walking; away from the lost lens, away from Flynn, away from the church, away from the lights of the bridge, farther into the cemetery, finding his way one drunken-eye blind.

Eric weaves through many pale white ghosts of gravestones, row after row. There's a dark shape ahead, the shape of a small building. He staggers to it slowly, trying not to slam into it, and reaches out to touch it. Cold rough stone. He walks around the building, finds a door, and goes inside, into deeper darkness. He sees a light grey square hovering in there, a window in the back of the room. Moving closer to the window, Eric sees blurry black tree branches waving in the wind outside. They look like skinny black arms and claws.

He's still a moment, listening to the wind and dry leaves blowing into the small dark stone room, then he moves to the side of the room and bumps into something on the floor. He takes a plastic cigarette lighter out of his jacket and flicks a little flame on. There's a long pale box on the floor, a gravestone at the top end. He puts the lighter away and it's dark again.

After a long moment standing still, Eric takes a careful step away from the box, finds a corner of the tiny room with his hands, and slides down to the floor, his legs splayed out in front of him. He buttons his jacket up all the way to his throat, hugs himself, and closes his eyes. He listens to the wind. He pulls his legs up to his chest, curling himself into a ball.

He listens to the wind and tries not to think about anything.

Eric looks out the window above him. He can see some of the tips of the branches in the window, blowing up and down in the wind. He wonders where he's dropped the beer. He has to piss, but he's too cold to move.

He wonders what time it is, and imagines the clock tower. He closes his eyes.

At the front of the church, candles are lit and his mother is playing a slow dirge on the organ. The organ is unbearably loud. Eric's family is crowded around the organ. Eric sits alone in the back row of the church, and his mother glares out at him as she plays the organ. A choir is crowded behind the family and they are moaning the slow dirge along with the organ. Eric watches his mother play the organ. He didn't know she could play. Coming to the end of the music now she raises her thin arms over her head, her hands like claws, and she looks out at Eric again. She sweeps her hands down onto the organ, attacking it, and holds the final note long and loud. She climbs up onto the organ stool, steps on top of the organ and lets out a horrifying scream. She stops screaming and starts crying. The family helps her down from the organ and they comfort her. Through it all, she never stops looking at Eric.

Silence except for the sound of his mother sobbing and moaning. Everyone turns from her to look at Eric. There are no expressions on their faces. They form a perfect line across the front of the church. The candles are blown out, one by one, by Eric's father, who has climbed out of a casket on the pulpit. Thin bones and rags of the suit he was buried in and his eyes bulge in his skull as he stares out at Eric. Eric is looking at those bulging eyes when the last candle is blown out.

It's dark in the church, except for a faint blue in the massive stained glass window high overhead. And it's quiet, except for the sound of feet shuffling on the floor, towards Eric.

There's whispering, and the voices get slowly louder. Eric is sitting in the dark at the back of the church and he tries to stand up, to get out, but he's hugging himself so tight and he has his legs entwined so tightly he can't move.

The voices are getting louder and clearer and the feet are marching, getting stronger and closer. The voices are chanting one word, and the feet are stomping out the syllables.

"Disappointed. Disappointed. Disappointed. Disappointed."

A long line of tiny candles floats down the aisle towards Eric. As they float closer, two tiny spots shine above each candle until the spots get close enough to Eric that he can see that these spots are *eyes* glaring into him and—*OH, whoa! Ok, ok, ok, ok, FUCK!*—Eric's arms fly out frantically looking for something to hold onto. He looks up into darkness, trying to focus on something. He inhales as though he's been underwater, and his eyes find the window with the branches waving outside; the branches moving gently now, the wind is down.

Eric exhales, and tries to get up off the floor and falls across the tomb. "Oh, sorry. Sorry there, lad. Beg your pardon, I'm on my way!" Eric pats the tomb lightly, stands up again, stumbles towards the door and through it, landing in the grass outside. He's on his feet right away.

"Ok Eric, let's go, let's get out of here! Fuck *me*!" He's staggering into the gravestones, so he stops and puts the broken glasses back on, squinting one eye. Ahead glow the lights of the bridge, so he fixes the one eye on that and starts walking.

Out of the cemetery now, breathing hard, he walks across the bridge and down into a dark and empty Cork. He looks around, trying to remember where to go, and turns left, hoping he's right.

Now he remembers where he is and how to get back to the Rose Lodge, so he slows down and looks at Cork as he walks along alone. He looks in the shop windows at the tea sets and hardware and guitars and fiddles and ironing boards and toys and wool sweaters and bottles of wine and vacations to Dublin. He looks up at the second-story bedrooms over the shops, imagining the lives up there. He comes to a home on the first floor where a kitchen window is open and stops. The window is open, a little smoke drifts out, he hears talking and frying. A man and woman are in there in robes, and they're frying something smoking on the oven; sounds and smells to Eric like sausages.

He passes a couple on the sidewalk, nods at them and they nod back. Eric walks around a corner and the Rose Lodge sign is glowing and swinging in the wind.

He walks to the front door and it's locked and dark inside, as he knew it would be, this late.

He digs down into his pockets for his room key, which also opens the front door, after hours. He can't find the key in any pocket. He closes his eyes and leans his head on the door.

As he stands there, his head on the door, wondering what to do next, he hears the latch slipping open inside. He steps back from the door, it opens, and Mary stands there, sleepy and smiling.

Eric moves back another step into the light of the Rose Lodge sign and Mary sees his red raw eyes and that he has only one lens in his glasses.

He stands stiff in the light like he's under arrest.

"Hello, Eric. I see you've got your pants on," she says. She puts a hand out to Eric. "The name's Mary. Come on in."

Eric steps inside as quietly as he can, shaking her hand, shaking his head.

"My name's Eric. Oh, you already know that. Ehm, *how* do you know that?" Mary shuts and locks the door.

"I like to know the name of my guests, you know. It's the personal touch."

Eric looks so bewildered looking out through his one good lens that Mary starts to laugh.

"This is your place, Mary?"

"I got hired today as manager. I had a good job interview, and he liked me. He gave me the job. Do you like the Beatles, by the way?"

Eric takes off his useless eyeglasses and looks around the lobby, still trying to figure this out and what to say next and thinking about his bed upstairs.

"I love the Beatles," he says. "*Ehm ...*" Mary, laughing again, takes his arm gently and leads him towards the stairway.

"Never mind, Eric, looks to me as if you've had a hard day's night, as they say. I think you need some sleep."

They tiptoe creaking up the stairs and come to the first-floor landing, near Eric's favorite painting from this morning, the one with the cottage and the pretty girl and his beautiful future.

"Are you from Kinsale too, Eric? I don't remember seeing you there."

"No, farther away. Limerick. I needed a change of scenery. A change of something, you know?"

Mary opens the door of his room and turns on the light.

"Yeah, me too Eric, I know. Rest well. Good night. See you at breakfast, then? Or are you doing something tomorrow?"

"I don't know what I'm doing tomorrow, Mary."

"Well, goodnight then."

Mary pulls the door shut and walks down the hall to her room. Eric opens the window and lets in the cold air. He falls on the bed and closes his eyes. He's almost asleep when he hears footsteps in the hall coming his way. Mary opens his door wide enough so she can see him in bed lit by the hallway light.

"You want a fuckin' job?"

"Well, yeah Mary, I would."

"Right. Assistant manager. Get some sleep."

And he does.

FROM THE HILLS above Cork, you can see the last lights go out in the Rose Lodge, though the sign in front is still lit and swings in the wind. And way over there, the clock dial at the top of the church tower glows yellow but you can't see the numbers from up here.

It's late. It's early.

A WARM FURRY SKULL

NEPO LIES on one of Sondra's old sweaters in a basket. His front paws are tucked in against his chest and his face is down deep into the smell of the sweater, the new smell of Sondra. He can smell her everywhere now, in these last couple of days. He sleeps with her smell in his nose and the wool of her sweater around his little slowly-breathing body. A little yellow nightlight glows nearby, lighting up his fur.

One of his ears goes up, hearing scratching. It's the scratching of other dogs in the shelter, reacting to the change of light in the shelter. The night is ending. The sun is coming. The scratching stops, and the dogs get up, circle and circle and drop, and go back to sleep. Nepo's ear drops.

He can feel Sondra's hand scratching his head, and he moves his head up into her hand so the scratching will last longer. When it stops he opens his eyes again and watches her hand go back into the blankets. Then he stands up and stretches all his legs out, shakes his head into a rhythm and gets his ears flapping, and drops back down into the sweater.

Nepo can feel the sun coming in through the window warming the top of his little furry skull.

THE SPEECH

THE SUN MOVES from the horizon into the pink and blue sky. Julie, awake all night, sits on the front porch, watches the dawn, and thinks. She's been thinking all night.

Julie's little dog Daisy sits on the porch looking around at everything with her one good eye. Daisy's blind eye is clouded over but her good eye focuses into the grass, watching for smaller animals. She's been there all night with Julie.

Julie reaches down for her bottle of wine and remembers yesterday's AA meeting. She pours wine into a glass and swings her bare feet onto the wooden railing of the front porch. She stretches out her legs and wiggles her toes. She's naked under her robe and now she pulls back the robe and lets the morning breeze blow down her legs.

She's thinking about the phone call she'd gotten last night, just before midnight. Her brother called from a hospital in London about their mother. He said she was dying. Julie laughed when he told her, but then she wondered if maybe her mother really was dying this time. She'd packed her bag and thrown it in the shuttle van.

The van is still sitting in the driveway. It hasn't moved an inch towards the road or the airport or London.

She's been thinking of all the times her mother has died over the years and all the almost funerals. When Julie had been caught having sex in an empty classroom with her first boyfriend her mother had almost "passed away." When she graduated from high school and made plans for a hitchhiking trip through Europe, her mother had an emergency visit to the emergency room and Julie canceled the trip. Julie's first marriage and divorce two years later had nearly killed her mother again, who cried for days; cried after the marriage ceremony and later after the divorce.

Julie doesn't remember her father being that kind of crier. He would cry without hesitation hearing almost any kind of music whether it was happy or sad, and he would weep freely on days of pain or joy. But he laughed as often and he would swing from sad to happy pretty fast. He was never stuck long in sadness.

Julie watched him watch people, she knew that he cared about those people—his family, his friends, and strangers. She'd seen him in pubs, restaurants, family holidays at the house, walking on the street. He'd be watching and wondering, sometimes worrying about people.

And he had been around and nearby always, it seemed to Julie, every day of her life. He was always asking, listening, laughing. He'd gotten very excited about her high school graduation. The day before the ceremony he had taken her to what he said was going to be a long lunch, which meant they were going to have some drinks, and he'd given her a present he'd gone all the way to Dublin to find.

Julie is wearing it this morning and she remembers her Dah taking the small, beautifully wrapped box from under the pub table and giving it to her.

She'd unwrapped and opened the box and inside was a large silver Celtic cross with a garnet stone shining red in the center. It was strung on a black cord that made her neck smell like leather for a long time after that day.

Julie's father had taken a bus to Dublin for this necklace. Before the trip, he'd asked around Cork about jewelry stores in Dublin. He wanted to know what the best one was, so when he got off the bus in Dublin he knew where to go in Temple Bar. He got to the corner of Grafton Street and Wicklow and walked in. He looked at almost everything in the store and then he saw the cross necklace, and he knew this was the gift for Julie. The young woman in the store wrapped the gift in delicate paper and red ribbons, humming and weaving the ribbons around the box and into a bow with graceful flourishes of her hands. Julie's father checked her name tag.

"You're very good at that, Isabel. It's gorgeous, what you're doing!"

"Thanks very much, sir."

"Sir? Call me what my friends call me." Isabel finished the wrapping and handed him the gift.

"And what do they call you then?"

"Rooster."

"And why is that, Rooster?" He took off his cap and his grey hair stood straight up. Isabel squinted at the big shock of hair standing up and laughed.

"I see, I see. Well, Rooster, how do you get your cap on? I'd say your hair has a mind of its own."

After Rooster paid Isabel, she came around the counter, gave him a hug and his hair a tousle, and escorted him out the door.

Out on the street, his graduation gift found and wrapped and in his pocket, the sun was out and everything seemed to be shining. He told Julie that everyone seemed to be smiling at him and saying hello. There was a busker outside the jewelry store who sang right to Rooster. It was a beautiful cold sunny day and Rooster wasn't sure he wanted to go home yet. He was feeling adventurous.

He had been worrying about catching the last bus back home but now he felt so good that he walked across the street and into a pub for fish and chips and a drink and he decided to stay in Dublin overnight. Somewhere. He'd maybe figure out where on the second drink.

The high school graduation ceremony was next Friday night and this was only Tuesday. And besides, he had his daughter's present already picked out, wrapped, and paid for. He was still working on a speech, the one he would deliver to her before the graduation ceremony, across the dining room table. So he'd have lunch and a drink or two, or three, then find a little hotel nearby and sleep. He'd catch the early bus and go home.

The sun glows down onto Julie, warming her up. She remembers her father telling her about that night in Dublin, thirty years ago.

That night, he told her, began at a corner table in the back of a pub, slowly ordering one drink, another drink, then another, and working on his speech. Around dark, Isabel had come in, looked over and waved at him, and sat down at the bar. She drank and flirted with the guys at the bar. They flirted with her too, but she kept looking back at Rooster. He was working on his speech, but he noticed Isabel looking at him and he waved her over.

After a few drinks and friendly small talk, she asked him what he was writing and he showed her what he had written so far. She took his pages and gently spread them out on the table, as gently as she had wrapped Julie's graduation gift. When she finished reading she was very quiet, keeping her eyes down on the pages, gently folding them together again and handing them back to him. Then she looked at him, stood up, leaned across the table, and kissed him on the forehead.

"You're a good Dah, Rooster. Let me buy you a drink!"

And soon the guys at the bar were sitting with Rooster and Isabel, and a little fiddle band sat down at the next table, and soon they were all clapping and singing. And in the middle of it all, Rooster took the speech out from time to time, adding sentences. Julie was very much on his mind in all this music and drinking and yelling and singing.

This all went on for hours; more drinks and more food, more songs, and then, somehow, it all came crashing down to silence. Glasses were cleared from tables, the band packed up their instruments and shook hands with Rooster, Isabel gave him a hug and a kiss, said goodbye, and everyone pulled up their collars and drifted out the door. And then Rooster was sitting at the table by himself, smiling and still singing. He leaned back in his chair, stretched his legs out, bumped something under the table, and a dog he hadn't noticed before ran off back behind the bar, part of a sandwich in his mouth.

Rooster took a last sip of his last drink and looked over at the barman whistling and cleaning up behind the bar. The clock over the bar read two o'clock.

He told Julie later that when he saw the time he laughed and said *uh-oh*. He stood up, wobbly, and walked out of the pub into the rain.

Outside, he saw a lot of dark windows, and started walking. There was a glowing light coming from a window down the street, a brightly lit furniture store window full of bedroom displays.

There were beds and blankets and bedside tables and lamps left on all night to show off the furniture for strolling window-shoppers. The bedside tables had fake family photos, and they were turned towards where someone would be sleeping. It would be the last thing someone would look at before turning off the bedside light and curling up under the blankets.

The bedroom displays in the window were brightly lit, but Rooster could see some further back in the dark.

He heard footsteps on the sidewalk so he pretended to be a window-shopper until the couple passed. He looked over his shoulder as they walked away into the dark and the rain.

Julie remembers him saying how cold he was then and how much he had to pee.

And there he was, looking at these warm, dry bedrooms behind the shop windows. He started singing again, laughing a little.

He walked around the building, down the alley, and stepped to a doorway behind the store. He turned around, leaned against the door, and pissed out into the alley. It was dark and the only other sound besides his pissing was the rain dripping down all around. He finished pissing, zipped up his pants, and saw through a window the bedroom displays in the back of the store, in the darkness, away from the sidewalk windows.

On the other side of the window. Rooster was freezing.

He pushed against the door, turned the doorknob, knowing it wouldn't open, and saw that there were many locks and signs about alarm systems, so he looked at the window. It didn't seem to be attached to any alarm wiring. At least there weren't any alarm stickers on it. It was an old window, an original one in the partly remodeled building, and he tried to lift it. It didn't lift but it didn't set off alarms either. He tried it again but it didn't move.

He leaned on the alley wall awhile, wondering what to do. He looked up into the sky and saw a radio tower, the little red light blinking through the fog at the top, and the rain was falling harder now. He checked his jacket pocket for his speech and gift to Julie, making sure they weren't getting wet. He found them safe and dry and turned around again to the window.

He hit it lightly and his hand just bounced off the glass. He picked up a piece of brick from the alley and hit it against the window but again it bounced back. He hit the glass harder. Two big shards of glass caved inside the window frame and broke on the floor. All of this was muffled by the rain coming down hard and he laughed at how small the sound of his breaking the window was. It hadn't been such a big deal. He picked out the leftover pieces of glass sticking from the window frame and pulled himself inside the window, into the store.

He checked that the rain was falling straight down, not blowing in the broken window. At least the rain wasn't coming in. He felt bad about breaking the window, but he was singing to himself again, and giggling.

Julie pours another glass of wine now, remembering this tale, and pulls little Daisy up onto her lap. Daisy looks up, then drops her head down on Julie's leg and falls back asleep. Julie shuts her eyes and sees her father's face again.

He walked softly through the dark store, making sure not to knock anything over. He found a bedroom display with the blanket already turned back. The bed was far from the brightly lit front window facing the street in a cozy hidden back corner of the store. He took off his jacket and laid it out neatly on the floor next to the bed.

He took his boots off and set them by his neatly folded jacket. Then he sank down gently into the bed and pulled the blanket over him. He had it in mind, he'd told her, not to mess up the sheets too much, so nobody would know that he'd been there, come morning. He'd just sleep, and slip back out through the broken window in the morning.

He'd leave some money and a note near the window for the broken glass, and he'd get his bus and go on home.

He told Julie later how he lay there peaceful and happy under the sheets and blankets, let his head sink back into the deep soft pillow, and how he listened to the rain coming down harder and harder outside the store and felt himself on a great adventure and safe inside the bed store.

From the bed, he looked out to the sidewalk where he'd been standing and freezing. He watched the rain fall beyond the store lights out on the street. The last thing he heard that night was the rain outside, and his last thoughts were about Julie.

It was the most peaceful sleep of his life, he'd told her.

Julie hears guests inside the inn and stands up, taking Daisy with her. She looks at the van, still sitting there going nowhere, and walks inside the inn. She starts slowly up the stairs and meets Kieran heading down. Sunlight is coming in a window from behind him and she can't see his face. Just the outline of his head.

Kieran brings his hand up and softly cups her cheek. He looks into her eyes. Something is going on.

"OK, come on," he says, and helps her up the stairs. They walk into their bedroom, and he takes off her robe. He eases her into bed and sits on the edge of the bed as she drops her head down into her dry, warm, fluffy pillow.

"Sleep," Kieran says to her. "Turn it all off," he says. "If she's really dead this time, then … she's really dead. And about time, eh, darling?" They both laugh and Kieran kisses her softly. He puts his warm hand on her forehead and says "Sleep." And Kieran walks out of the room, shutting the door softly, as softly as he had touched her forehead.

Julie lies in bed with the blankets up to her chin. She closes her eyes and listens to the wind creak the wood in the walls of the inn. The wind rattles a loose glass pane in the window.

Julie listens to the wind and window and remembers the rest of her father's story.

In the morning, the manager of the bed store came and found Rooster in one of the best, most expensive beds and called the police. Rooster slept through this, so later, it was the police who woke him. The two policemen came into the store, asked the manager what was going on, where the burglar was, and when they saw Julie's father, started to laugh. They walked over to him and gently squeezed his arm to wake him. This startled Rooster so much that he jumped out of bed, knocking a bedside lamp to the floor and almost knocking over one of the policemen. The policemen tried to steady him as he began apologizing and pulling out his wallet and pulling his pants up and putting his hat on and picking up the broken lamp, all somehow at the same time.

"If I'd only been awake a wee five minutes earlier," Rooster told Julie later.

"I'm so sorry, sir, I'll make it right, I will," he said, as one policeman helped him pick up the broken glass. The other policeman began making up the bed, chuckling to himself about the mess. They wanted to clean everything up, see that Rooster paid the manager for damages, and get him out of there. But the manager insisted on *arrest*.

Rooster held out a lot of cash to the manager and even recommended a hardware store and glass shop he knew of. He said he'd measure the window himself, go to the store and buy the glass, glazing, bring it back and put it in. The policemen listened to this offer then turned to the store manager and nodded.

"A good offer, sir," one of them had said. "He's tryin' to make it right, why don't you go easy with him?" Rooster felt so grateful to the policemen for this, he felt that everything was going to be alright after all (as he stood there holding out his wallet of cash with one hand, his unbuckled pants up with the other).

The bed store manager insisted on arrest. He insisted that Julie's father be "brought to justice."

The policemen looked at the manager. Then they walked Rooster out of the store. They didn't put the cuffs on him and they didn't take him by the arm. They held the door for him and said, "Let's get the hell out of here, sir."

One of them turned back to the store manager and said, "Bring him to justice. Is that it? Is that what you're wanting? You're watching too much television news, mate."

The three left the store and as they walked along in the general direction of the police station, one of the policemen asked Julie's father what his name was.

"Rooster," he told them, and when they didn't say anything he took off his cap.

"Oh, I see."

When they finally "arrested" him later, after a leisurely breakfast together, they escorted him to a cell and sat in there with him. They wanted to hear him read his graduation speech. They listened to him read it all the way through and then they called down the hall and the other policemen came in and listened to Rooster's speech as he read it aloud again.

They all had ideas and suggestions, and Rooster crossed out lines and wrote down new ones. He tried to keep up with all the ideas coming from his jail cell full of policemen.

At last, he read one they could all agree on, and they stood up and applauded him.

"THAT'S the one, now you've got it!" And then the policemen drifted out of his cell and back down the hall, each of them shaking his hand on the way out. The two policemen who'd "arrested" him stayed to the last. One of them brought him tea, and left the cell door open.

"What time's the next bus then, Rooster?"

And, a couple of hours later, when they dropped Rooster off at the station, they'd told him, "Give her a good speech or we *will* come and arrest you!"

They laughed and waved to him as the bus drove out of the Dublin station.

Julie remembers that these two policemen had come to her father's funeral last year. They stood up together and told the story of his so-called arrest and everyone laughed. Or almost everyone. Her mother glowered and glared, crossed and uncrossed her legs, sighed a lot, and when her turn came to say some words about her husband, and she didn't call him Rooster, she began by remarking on how "inappropriate" the arrest stories were for the occasion. She glowered and glared some more at the policemen in the front row who looked down at their hats in their laps. Then she said some things about his being a good provider and how long he'd stuck with his job and how he'd been promoted twice and had been given pay raises both times. And then something about his good character, although, she said, "he would get a bit wild at times, and sometimes get a little loud." She said that she didn't understand the necessity of this when he had such a nice personality when he was just being himself.

"But I know that there will be stars in your crown now my dear darling husband, now that you're at last in eternal rest, and not fighting life anymore." Julie remembers looking over at the policemen who were either confused by this last remark or trying not to laugh.

And, of course, her mother went on.

"And I do know my dear that you loved me as I loved you. Rest in peace, my dear. No more pain, my dear. No more restlessness or resistance in your poor tortured soul. Acceptance is everything darling, as I have always tried to tell you, and so now rest forever in God's arms."

Julie sits up in bed and hears the wind again and she smiles. It's her father's smile. What one of the policemen called "A troublemaker smile. A trickster smile. A friendly smile. A smile of the pub and of the wide-open countryside." She remembers the night her father gave his speech.

It was the evening before the graduation ceremony at her school. He had told her during their long lunch to meet him and her mother at the kitchen table at six o'clock. The house smelled like his stew all day. This stew being the one thing he could cook, his wife liked to say, that didn't come from a box with directions. She said it again that day.

At six o'clock, Julie and her mother sat down at the table. Rooster walked into the kitchen with a black leather journal and sat down at his place at the table.

He was wearing a clean white shirt and a tie Julie'd never seen before. It looked new. It was red with little yellow chickens on it. He had tried his best to comb his hair back neatly, but it did have a mind of its own. She could smell his shaving lotion. He was smiling and seemed a bit nervous. He opened the journal and began to read his speech.

He talked about things Julie had long forgotten. He talked about drawings she'd made and tiny clay sculptures and how fast and good she was with the piano lessons and the day she saved the soccer game when she dived sideways and blocked the ball. And how, after, she still looked beautiful, even covered in goalie mud.

He remembered everything she'd ever done and it all was in the speech.

Then he talked a bit about his trip to Dublin and Isabel and how the police there thought she was pretty grand as well, and how they'd told him they'd come and arrest him if he didn't give a good speech for such a wonderful daughter.

And now she remembers the last lines of her father's graduation speech. The speech written on a bus, in a bar, in a *broken-into* bed store on a rainy night, and in a jail cell with the help of seven Dublin policemen. She knows these last lines are all his. She has them memorized.

Julie darling. My sweet darling daughter. I have some soft advice for you. Look out your window. Open your window. Listen to the wild wind. Listen to the water in the streams and in the lakes and in all our surrounding seas. Listen to the way the night sounds outside your window, listen to the rain. Listen to music and listen to yourself when you hear music. Listen to other people and listen to yourself as you hear them. There's never been a one like you. I'll always listen for you on the wind and on the water and it'll all always be the best music for me. I love you, Julie. Well done, daughter. Well done.

Julie gets out of bed and walks over to the window. She opens it and the wind flies in, chilling her naked body. She stands in the window and her hair flies back. She feels the cold wind on her body and listens to the wind blow across the room scattering magazines off the bedside table and knocking over her perfume bottles.

She's still smiling, a little bigger now, when she says, "This is some wind, Dah. Is it you I'm hearing now? Is this your so-called poor tortured soul blowing in my window? Is this your poor tortured soul about to knock me and my perfume bottles across the room? Is this what you call resting forever in God's arms?"

A car comes down the road and slows a little in front of Kieran's Inn. The driver looks curiously at the inn as he passes then glances up to Julie standing naked and smiling in the upstairs window, her hair blowing wildly.

Julie watches the car swerve, raise a burst of dust, right itself back onto the road, and speed away.

She closes the curtains on the open window and gets back into bed. Daisy, afraid of the wind, is under the covers already sleeping. Julie smells the wet wind blowing in through the flapping curtains and burrows herself down warm into the sheets, under the blankets.

"Good night, Rooster. Goodbye, mother."

SENSE AND INSENSIBILITY

ROB WAKES UP and looks across his bed to the bedside table at the red zero on his telephone answering machine. Don't do it. Don't start this. Don't start thinking, he thinks.

It's dark in his room except for that red zero. Rob looks up and the ceiling is faintly glowing red from the zero. And he thinks, alright Rob, here it comes—the big symbol of this moment. You're good at this sort of drama. The big red zero in the empty dark room and me all alone. The morning after a good day when I was really *out there*, and nobody has called, nobody has noticed. Don't make it a symbol. Don't take it the wrong way. Don't do what you always do in your mind. Tommy hasn't called and nobody else has called. Chester hasn't phoned. This doesn't mean they've written you off and forgotten you.

The big red zero is a big zero in significance.

Rob likes this line. He sits up in bed and writes it down in his bedside notebook with his favorite plastic blue ballpoint pen, the one he can buy at the liquor store on the corner. He likes it that his favorite pen is one he can buy in any train station or market or airport. They all have this pen for less than a euro, and he can always buy it and make literature on the spot, anywhere. Make himself make sense. He's doing it now, by writing it down.

He had a dream last night but it's mostly faded away. Until he begins remembering, and then he remembers more and more. He remembers that he had been on the ground in the dream, this recurring dream, and he's crouching down, people standing over him, laughing at him. He starts to write this down but decides to forget it instead because it's boring now, this old dream that goes nowhere.

Rob puts the notebook down and gets out of bed, walks into the kitchen. The kitchen window lets in white morning light across the sink. He switches on a yellow-shaded lamp on his wooden dining table, lights his oven, and opens his refrigerator door. He pulls out a jug of milk and an egg and opens a box of soda bread mix. Rob spoons and swirls it all together in a bowl and scoops it out into a square tin and slides it into the oven.

He takes down a pewter breakfast tray from the wall, which was a pewter drink tray from Tommy's bar. Tommy gave it to him as a present for his new home. He puts on the tray a butter knife, a plate, a tea cup, and a cream pitcher. He has one each of these things, and they're all on the tray. Rob starts the pot boiling for tea and walks back into his dark bedroom. He gets back into bed and looks at the bedside clock to time his bread. He can smell it now and he can hear the pot of water beginning to steam on the stove. Light comes in around the edges of the curtains and he hears feet crunching on the street outside. Alex the cat has been somewhere else in the apartment all night, but now he jumps on the bed and drops down into the folds of the bedspread and blankets, sensing food and cream and company.

In a few minutes, Rob will have tea and warm fresh bread with butter slathered on top and he'll give Alex his little saucer of cream. They'll have breakfast in bed. Then Rob will get up and get dressed, take more of the promotional flyers, and go find Tommy.

The red zero of the answering machine is invisible now as the room begins to lighten up.

Fuck symbols, Rob thinks. Fuck that dream. Fuck thinking too, he thinks.

"But as long as I'm still thinking," he says to Alex, "I think I'll just *change* my thinking."

Alex hears him, drops his head to his paws, and closes his eyes.

Rob says, "Everything's going to be alright now."

CHESTER HANGS UP ON AMERICA

CHESTER IS BACK in his blue corduroy robe again this morning, up the hill in his stone house, looking out the window. He's had a phone call from back home in America and it was a short one and now the telephone is out in the yard in the rain.

The call was pretty much the usual kind, the normal one, the predictably mean one, starting quiet ending loud with the yelling and the criticism and the questions and finally the crying, and since he wants no more of this sort of normal, the telephone is now in the grass, black plastic broken in two.

"Try calling me on *that*," he says.

And after a few more minutes of loud yelling and laughing and kicking things and feeling great about hanging up and flinging the phone out the window, he stops and pulls the phone back towards the house by its cord. He pulls it back to the house, hauls it up by the cord inside the window, but the two pieces of phone get no dial tone.

So be it, he says to himself.

Chester gets dressed, slams the door, and is off to Kieran's.

TOMMY WARMING UP

TOMMY IS ALSO AWAKE early this morning. He's been awake all night.

The sun coming up, he's begun his new day with a bath and a shave and sausages and tea (with lemon, for the voice) and vitamins even, and he has on his lucky leather coat. This is the coat he'd worn on the Irish Sea that night, singing on the ferry. He's put the coat on for strength. He's put it on for protection from music teachers. From critics.

He's pacing around his flat from the bathroom mirror to the living room window and back to the bathroom mirror again. He likes how he looks in the mirror and smiles at himself. He takes his cup of tea off the sink, steps into the shower stall where he sings some scales, and right away someone next door starts knocking on the wall.

"Right, sorry!" He steps back out and yanks the shower curtain shut. "And anyway," he winks at himself in the mirror, "I'm through with that 'singing in the shower' gig, I'm all done with working *that* room."

Tommy goes to the phone, dials a number, and smiles now, listening to his friend.

"Could you repeat that, I'd like to write it down." Tommy takes a pen out of his lucky coat and starts writing on a tablet of paper. "And who said that? Paddy Maloney? Paddy Maloney, The Chieftains? Jesus. What a line. Thanks, Rob. See you."

Tommy sits quietly at the table and reads what he's written. He looks out at the tops of some of the buildings of Cork through the window. Sunlight comes in and out of the clouds and onto the buildings and it's very windy out there this morning.

Groups of pigeons fly by and yellow leaves are whirling around in the blue and cloudy sky.

Tommy's staring out at Cork and he's smiling, tears in his eyes. He's just heard something that his brain couldn't get to all night long lying in bed, thinking and thinking and thinking and thinking and thinking.

He looks again at the line he's written down—

I'D RATHER DO SOMETHING WELL

THAN BADLY, AND I'D RATHER

DO SOMETHING BADLY

THAN NOT AT ALL.

— Paddy Maloney

The sun breaks all the way free of the clouds, shines off the building across the street from Tommy's building and bounces back across the street into his room. It's warmer and brighter in the room and a pigeon lands in his window, sits down next to the cup of tea he's left on the sill. The pigeon looks at Tommy, pecks at the side of the teacup with a tiny clink, flies away.

On the table is a stack of magazines, famous musicians and singers and actors and politicians and rich people talking about how they did it, and so on. Tommy takes out a thin cigar, lights it, and lights the stack of magazines.

He stands up, takes an old album out of the record shelf (a Guinness crate from the pub, hung on the wall), drops it down onto the spindle of his record player, and watches it spin. The record is *Astral Weeks* and he's counting over to the next to the last track on the second side, "Ballerina." Tommy drops the needle gently and after some pops and cracks, he hears the vibraphone and the guitar and the brushes on the drums and then Van Morrison's voice.

And now it's time to go sing somewhere, *out there*.

He drops the burning magazines in the bathtub, leaves the flat, and leaves Van, singing—

"... spread your wings ... come on, fly awhile..."

OVER THE TOPS OF THE BUILDINGS

THERE'S ANOTHER ONE AWAKE this morning in Cork, but he's not singing.

Declan came to his office this morning to check his appointment book, knowing it was empty before he came in to check it; looking at his telephone answering machine for messages, knowing it would be the same thing, empty. No mail from his father either. He's closed his empty office and now he's walking along the street thinking about business, and he has no business.

Walking along this morning, he's not sure what he's doing in Cork.

He walks along slowly this morning, and he watches people hurrying to places, hurrying to work, going to breakfast. He doesn't feel the inspiration to hurry anywhere, to go anywhere. He feels that there's nothing to do at all.

The sun breaks out of the clouds and slides back in behind them again. It's grey and windy, and Declan pulls his jacket collar higher. He stops in front of a hardware store and looks at himself in the glass reflection. He hasn't spoken to anyone in days now. He feels himself lowering into a hole he doesn't think he has the energy to climb out of at all.

Here we go again, he thinks.

He wonders why his father and mother haven't checked on him here. He wonders why he hasn't spoken to anyone here; he'd dreamed of this city for so long in his loneliness at the Killarney Holiday Inn. He'd driven here and gotten so excited seeing the lights of the Cork skyline that night.

He turns around and watches people hurrying along the street and they all seem happy, with places to go. A toothless homeless man wrapped in a green woolen blanket sitting in a doorway across the street strums a guitar and sings. The body of his guitar is beautifully polished wood and all the strings are there and the man sings right on key and with a fearlessness that Declan can't quite understand or touch in this moment. The man looks across the street at Declan, smiles his toothless smile and keeps on singing. Declan hadn't heard him a moment ago, but now the man's voice fills Declan's head. He turns around to look at his reflection again, and there's a short, husky man pulling back a little curtain and laying out new screwdrivers and hammers in his window display. The man takes his time and arranges them in neatly spaced rows, turning the little paper price tags up, and smoothing out the red felt display cloth. He looks up at Declan and mouths *good morning* through the glass. Then the man is gone and the little curtain falls back, and it's just the screwdrivers and the hammers and Declan looking at himself in the glass. And there's something different in his face. Just a minute or two, just a couple of other people, and something has changed in him. Still looking at himself in the glass, he also sees the guitar player again, over his shoulder behind him, across the street, and he hears that voice. Declan turns around.

The man's hands are raw and red in the cold, one hand precise on the neck of the guitar, the other hand slashing away at the strings. The man sits on a white bucket, his body still and anchored, both feet tapping out the rhythm. The man leans back, chest out, and drops his head back when he sings, opening up his throat and voice box and lungs and heart and soul (Declan feels all that coming out), and the voice goes up the sides of the buildings and above them into the sky.

Declan thinks about how dead his own voice has become.

People are dropping coins into the man's beat-up, elegant black fedora, and the man doesn't miss a note as he nods thanks to them.

Declan looks down the street to the window of what is his office, up at the top of an old building. That little window, that little office.

A small crowd is gathering around the singer across the street and people are singing with him. The hardware store door opens and the short husky man comes out onto the sidewalk to listen to the music. He's smiling at the singing, looks at Declan and gives him the thumbs-up sign, goes back into his store. It's even windier now and the wind brings the smell of bread down the street. The smell of bread, perfume, sour beer, meat frying somewhere.

The morning for Declan is gradually getting louder, larger, and is somehow slowing down. Since arriving in Cork he has been looking at the sidewalk and avoiding faces, moving fast and hiding in his office. And then in the office, thinking of making phone calls but mostly waiting for the phone to ring, knowing it won't.

Now he is *seeing* Cork.

He watches as the singer closes his eyes, opens his mouth, and leans back, singing up over the tops of the buildings.

Declan turns again to the little window down the street, his office. It seems smaller now and seems to get farther and farther away.

Declan stares unblinking down the street at the office window, wondering. The wondering has started and it has come from *somewhere,* he doesn't know *where* it came from, but it's growing. He feels it more than he understands it, but as it grows it becomes bright and focused.

He still hears the music and he's thinking of the rent on the office, the computer and the office equipment and the furniture, and the deposit money his father will lose if Declan follows the wondering.

Declan blinks out of his thoughts, smiles, takes a twenty euro note out of his wallet, walks across the street and drops it in the singer's hat. The singer, still singing, looks down from the sky to the blue euro note in his dusty hat. Then he looks up at Declan, who smiles and walks away. For the first time, the singer goes suddenly and briefly off-key, but he doesn't stop singing.

Declan walks down the street, *away* from his office. Smaller and farther away.

The office window, not Declan.

And as Declan walks, he looks down at pieces of wet paper, all in the same handwriting. They're all plastered down wet with footprints. He bends down and peels one off the street.

**CORK HAS A NEW VOICE!
THE SONGBIRD HAS FLOWN
AND ITS NAME IS
TOMMY LALLY!!!!**

At the bottom of the piece of muddy paper, there's a phone number and a name written down small. The name is Rob. Declan folds the paper into a little square and puts it in his jacket pocket. He doesn't know why he's saving this piece of paper. Normally he would drop it back on the street. He doesn't know why, but it's been kind of a musical morning.

It's been kind of an interesting morning in general, in Cork.

DELICATE LIFE

NEPO WALKS OUT into the yard of the animal shelter to lie down with the other dogs.

There's an old yellow dog named Bonnie in a corner of the yard, and she lifts her nose into the wind, peering into the sky, watching birds and leaves flying over. She has clear, alert brown eyes that gleam gold in the sun. She's alone in the corner, she's been there more and more over the past few days. The other dogs look at her from a distance and leave her alone.

Bonnie moves herself around the yard by her two front legs, her back legs dragging behind her dead and rubbed raw in the dirt. She moves around in circles, trying to find a way to sit that doesn't hurt her and can't, and she pees down those limp legs. As she drags herself across the yard she leaves a damp, brown smear behind her. Her eyes continue to shine as she eagerly looks around her world getting smaller.

A woman comes to the little window in the shelter fence and calls to the dogs. They all rush over to her, barking, and Bonnie tries to get to her as well. She drags herself a few yards, barking and crying, and finally falling over onto her side, out of breath and peeing on herself again. After a moment, the woman walks away down the sidewalk, along the fence, and Bonnie follows her with her eyes, breathing hard. When the woman walks out of sight behind a building, Bonnie looks around the yard, and up at the sky. Then she drags herself back to the corner.

Nepo stands in the middle of the yard watching Bonnie. His ears go up and he wags his tail when he sees Sondra come out of the shelter, but he walks away from her slowly seeing what she's carrying. She has something silver and sharp with a long black cord trailing behind her and it scares Nepo. He walks away from her, to one side of the yard. He stands shivering, staring at a wall.

Bonnie sees Sondra coming, lifts her head and barks once. She pulls herself towards Sondra, eyes shining and bright and yearning. Her dead tail and crippled legs drag behind her. Sondra sits down beside Bonnie and gathers the old dog into her lap. She strokes Bonnie's head and gives her a chunk of chicken breast, which the old dog chomps and swallows down, looking up into Sondra's eyes for more. Sondra has no more chicken, and her hands are shaking as she fumbles with the electric razor and the hypodermic needle.

She lays them out side by side on a small blanket on the ground and goes back to stroking Bonnie on the head, along her back, down along the dead legs. Sondra thinks about all the final things; the last night of sleep, the last morning waking up, the last sound of barking, the last piece of chicken, and her shoulders are shaking.

The other dogs stand around watching, standing silently in a kind of haphazard circle, surrounding Sondra and Bonnie. Nepo keeps staring at a wall, listening.

"I love you so much, dear Bonnie. Thank you for being such a wonderful dog. Thank you for being my friend, my very dear friend. I'm so glad that I found you and that you were here with me all this time." Sondra leans down and hugs the dog's head against her face, stroking her body. Bonnie gives her a small lick on the cheek and as Sondra sits up again the dog looks at her hands for more chicken or more petting. Sondra's hands are on the electric razor now.

Bonnie doesn't see any chicken and she looks around the yard, up at the sky again, looking with her bright brown eyes, taking everything in. But she is shaking a little now, and she looks around more frantically.

Sondra takes one of the limp rear legs in her hands, brushes off some dirt and bits of dried blood, and strokes it a moment longer. Then she clicks the electric razor on humming, delicately shaves off an inch of fur, turns off the razor. Bonnie, cradled in Sondra's lap, looks up into *sky* with her eyes very wide, and she looks into Sondra's eyes. The dog breathes hard with her long pink tongue hanging out of her mouth and her nose twitching, smelling the chemicals. Sondra looks down into Bonnie's mouth, little bits of chicken in her teeth. She whispers goodbye and very gently finds the vein in the dog's rear leg with the needle. Sondra feels Bonnie stiffen with the needle in her and the old dog tries now to stretch her head up towards Sondra, to get closer to her somehow. Her eyes are very wide now and looking into Sondra's eyes with a kind of panic or a question. She's trying so hard to get up closer to Sondra if she can. One of her front paws softly comes up into the air in front of Sondra's face and then falls back onto her chest. The dog slowly softens in Sondra's arms and exhales heavily with a grumbling moaning. Bonnie folds down limp into Sondra's lap, her eyes still open and rotating around trying to understand or see something, looking up past Sondra into the sky. Still shining golden and bright in the sunlight.

Sondra's got her stethoscope on Bonnie's chest listening. A little tip of pink tongue hangs out of Bonnie's mouth.

Sondra is crying with the dead limp body of the dog in her lap.

"Thank you," she says to the open eyes. "Thank you for trying so hard always to be a good, friendly dog. I'll always remember you and love you for that."

Sondra remembers the day Bonnie came to the shelter years ago, pretty much thrown in the door of the shelter by the brutal drunken former owner, the *puppy* Bonnie, looking back and forth from her owner to the stranger Sondra, trying to please somebody.

Sondra softly rolls Bonnie onto a pink blanket on the ground and tucks her legs and tail in close to her body. She drapes a long red scarf with a pattern of roses over Bonnie's body, and walks quickly back inside the shelter.

The other dogs move in close and smell the scarf, then drift off around the yard in different directions and lie down.

Nepo settles himself down into a ball near the wall and closes his eyes.

THE SONGBIRD FLIES,
A MEAN BLACK PIANO WATCHES

AN OLD BLACK SCRATCHED-UP PIANO sits framed in the middle of a pub window in Cork. The piano is positioned so that the keys are facing out the window, into the street. So that the piano player will be right there in the window, bringing in customers, the idea seems to be. The piano is old and the keys are yellow playing towards brown, and the piano, situated like this, looking out into the street like this, seems like a dangerous old black dog with bad teeth, guarding the pub.

That's what Rob thinks, anyway.

And he thinks he'd better write that line down, but he doesn't. He's busy; he's thinking. He's standing across the street, looking at the piano, waiting for the pub to open in a few minutes. It's morning, and in the morning, Rob always has plans. He has had them *all day*, lately. He smiles at that piano with some sort of plan in the smile. He hears whistling coming down the street, but he doesn't look away from the piano yet. He doesn't even look away from the piano when he recognizes the whistling, but the smile gets a little more so and more plans seem to arrive in the smile as the whistler gets closer. Still, he doesn't look away from the mouth of the piano until Tommy is standing right in front of it, across the street. And then Rob looks at Tommy, who's smiling back at him. Tommy starts to say something, has his mouth open to say it and even his finger up in the air to help him say it, and then he drops it all, and drops his hand. He doesn't drop the smile, though. Rob is looking past him at the piano again and his smile is so big now that it almost mirrors the piano keyboard across the street. Brown teeth and all.

That's what Tommy thinks, anyway.

"Can you play that?" asks Rob. Tommy looks behind him.

"That?" Tommy uses his talking finger to point at the piano.

"Yeah, that."

"No."

Rob hears that and of course the answer makes a silence in the air between them for a moment but it takes away neither Rob's smile nor, it seems, his plans.

"Doesn't matter, doesn't matter." Rob starts to say something else but Tommy stops him.

"I'm singing today."

"Are you? Where, Tommy? When?"

Tommy starts singing. Not words, really, just tones, notes, his head back, his thumbs in his front belt loops, and his eyes closed. Rob hasn't heard him like this before, and he leans against the brick building on the other side of the street. He looks puzzled, like this wasn't part of his plans somehow. But he likes it. He looks around to see if someone else is around and hearing Tommy.

The barman of the piano pub comes outside in his grey wool cap and white apron and watches Tommy. He looks across at Rob and they both shake their heads. A skinny old man in a brown suit and white whiskers peaks out of the alley beside the pub. He breaks off what he is doing in the alley, you might say that he *shakes* it off, and he comes out to listen to Tommy sing, zipper still open. And his mouth is open. He likes the singing so much he sort of straightens up and pulls the lapels of his jacket together, brushes them off, buttons a couple of buttons. He slicks back his greasy hair on both sides of his head; the singing is so good that he takes off his cap, takes out a comb, actually combs his top hairs straight back neatly, and he holds the cap respectfully across his chest.

"Good, isn't he?"

The old man turns to the voice by his side. Declan leans close to the old man.

"By the way, your fiddle case is open," Declan motions to the old man's fly and goes on listening to Tommy. The old man holds his cap over his zipper with one hand, and struggles to zip it up with the other.

The street in front of the pub is full of people now and in the window, by the piano, the cook and the dishwasher and the waiters all stand in a line of smiles, watching Tommy.

"Is this the songbird?" asks the young man with the folded paper. The old man is still fiddling with his zipper, which has gotten stuck halfway.

Suddenly, he jerks hard on the zipper and rips his pants open.

Declan looks at the old man who is looking down at a big hole ripped in his crotch, exposing part of a skinny white bony leg. Declan looks down at the hole too.

There's a bit of a pause. The two men look at each other for a moment. They hear Tommy singing again and look away from each other to watch Tommy. Then they both look back down at the hole in the pants. The old man smiles, then begins laughing, though he tries to hide it from Declan, who is turning red, his cheeks puffed out full, also trying to hide his laughing.

"Maybe he *is* the songbird," says the old man, looking down at his crotch again. "*This* bird hasn't sung in years. Got the price of a pint?" asks the old man, letting out his laughter now, holding his cap over his hole. Declan laughs now too, and they join the crowd in the street, clapping to Tommy, singing along with Tommy, who is singing "Dicey Reilly."

Tommy stands on a bus stop bench a bit above the crowd, leaning forward, one hand on his hip, the other hand leading the singing, his chest puffing up full with every new breath pouring out full into the next lyric, and in the middle of all this, a boy on the side of the crowd kicks a soccer ball at Tommy who catches it and kicks it over his head and keeps on singing, and the boy looks up at Tommy and stares and stares and stares and then he smiles.

The boy hasn't seen a man like *this* before.

"Oh aye, I've got the price of a pint," Declan says, clapping and laughing harder now than he has, maybe, ever. He looks down at the old man's cap.

"And I've got the price of a pant as well!"

The old man laughs but now he's looking at something, and very focused. He gazes past Declan to the piano in the bar window.

"I can play that, you know," he says to Declan, suddenly serious. He puts his hat on, exposing himself again, and begins fingering a piano in the air in front of him. Declan watches this for a few respectful but curious moments, then he breaks out laughing again.

Across the street, Rob watches them.

"Go on laugh, you'll see," the old man squawks at Declan, punching him in the arm with his bony right hand. "Let's get in there, I'll back him up, I know this song, come on," and the old man cuts through the crowd, Declan following.

Tommy has finished his song, and the crowd applauds and begins to break apart. Men and women are coming to Tommy, the men shaking his hand, the women hugging him and, some of them, crying. As Declan and the old man come near they hear one of the men say "Wonderful singin' there Tommy, you just keep on with it and you'll be out of that pub apron yet!"

Declan, looking around for the old man, says, "It *is* Tommy." But the old man has made his way up to the front door of the pub and tries to get inside to play the piano. The waiters try to slow him down but the pub is open for business and the crowd is moving towards the door, and the old man is swept inside. Very soon he is at the keyboard of the old black piano with a glass of stout; he takes a long, long drink of the beer, sets it on top of the piano, and cracks his knuckles. His hands over the keys, he hesitates, and then he takes another drink of beer.

Rob watches from across the street as Declan takes the folded piece of paper from his pocket, unfolds it, and walks up to Tommy. Tommy reads it, laughs, and points at Rob.

"My manager," says Tommy. Declan looks across the street.

"Oh, is that Rob?" Rob stays where he is. Declan smiles and nods at Rob, looks back at Tommy.

"Anyway, you were great! Where do usually sing? I mean, what is the standard venue for your, you know, your ... where you *sing?* Did your manager set up this concert?"

Tommy can see this man is even greener than he is in the music business, if he *is* in the music business. If either one of them is. But Tommy notices that Rob is frowning, and he's never seen him frown. And just as Tommy is about to answer Declan, there is the crashing sound of a piano falling down a long stairway, or maybe out of a window into the street. Tommy and Declan both crouch, arms over their heads, and spin around, squinting.

The old man has begun playing the piano.

Tommy and Declan stand back up.

"I just started singing," Tommy says, and he feels the power of what he's just said. So he says it again. "I just started singing."

Rob slowly walks across the street. Tommy smiles and watches him come. The songbird *has* flown, he's thinking.

Declan watches the old man at the piano. The old man is very busy at the piano. His left hand, an angry claw, continues to pound out the low thunder and lightning notes while his right goes to the top of the piano for his glass of stout again. He toasts the crowd in the pub, drops the glass on the floor, returns his right hand to the high keys and it sounds like flocks of panicked birds flying away from the thunder and lightning.

None of this sounds much like music, of course.

But the old black piano shakes and jars closer to the front window of the pub.

Rob stands next to Tommy, but he's looking at Declan. Still frowning.

DELICATE TRUST

NEPO DROWSILY WAKES UP in the corner of the shelter yard, still facing the wall. Night is coming, and he's been sleeping in the corner all day.

He looks over his shoulder to the empty yard and doesn't even get up to stretch. It is lightly raining, and the other dogs have gone inside to their little pens. Nepo hears the loud sound of an idling truck engine in the alley, a sound that usually gets him all glassy-eye-wild and sends him running and barking against the alley wall. He sees that the door to the alley is open as the trash man goes in and out of the yard to the trash truck. He hears the familiar voice of the trash man talking in the alley, and the door lingers open.

Nepo stands up slowly and blinks. He still doesn't stretch and his tail hangs down. He walks over to the spot where Bonnie died and dips his head down to sniff the spot. Then he starts walking again, the little legs working slowly, towards the open alley door, his tail and his head hanging down.

When he gets to the alley door he pauses and looks down to where the trash man is talking and laughing with someone. He looks at them, then turns and walks in the other direction. When he gets near the big noisy trash truck, Nepo walks as close against the alley wall as he can, away from the truck, away from the vibrating engine noise and smoke. He sees the opening of the alley into the street and many people and cars crossing back and forth. He stops for a moment and looks back behind him down the alley. He doesn't want to go near that truck again, so he walks towards the street.

When he gets to the sidewalk he begins to tremble and he keeps his eyes low. His eyes flick back and forth watching the feet crossing both ways on the sidewalk. He stops and waits, not sure where to go.

He hears a shrieking behind him. He turns and looks down the alley. The big truck flashes white lights and backs up towards him. Nepo barks once frantically but feels the big thing vibrating nearer to him and he smells the gasoline smoke again. He runs out onto the sidewalk, ducking down low into all those feet. He skitters over close to a wall and his little paws cautiously step one at a time to move him along away from the feet on the sidewalk. He keeps as near to that wall as he can. Nepo keeps his head down but his eyes look up very timidly at the faces high above him.

Nepo comes to another alley and turns into it quickly, stops and leans against a wall, his chest rising and falling, out of breath. His tongue hangs out and he drops his head down and licks the moisture on the paving stones of the alley. He looks back towards the street, still breathing hard, then walks softly down the alley, away from the noise and all those feet on the sidewalk. His head and tail still hanging low as he walks.

He comes to a stack of boxes near the end of the alley and finds a tattered grey blanket bunched up behind the stack. Nepo begins to paw it into a nest, and drops down, exhaling. The blanket is wet and Nepo continues to shiver, but it's quiet here and he's nestled in his nest, safe for now behind the boxes.

Nepo drops his head down onto the puffed-up soft ridge of the blanket and falls asleep.

In his sleep, Nepo hears a wet crash somewhere and he wakes up as a bird falls to the alley floor right in front of him. The bird's wings twitch and try to fly, as the eyes of the bird turn over and the eyelids close, turning white. The delicate feet of the bird reach and claw at the air, and Nepo is so close he can see the tiny nails on its feet.

Nepo is trembling again. He stares at the bird. There is some movement in the wings, the eyelids damp, and the head of the bird lies on the pavement, with the beak towards Nepo. The beak opens and closes quietly. Nepo looks away. He gets up, turns around and around in circles and drops down again, facing away from the bird, towards the alley wall, and sleeps.

Nepo jerks awake to the shrieking sound again. There's a bright flash of light across the alley wall right in front of him, and he feels the heavy, noisy vibration coming towards him. He stands up quickly and shakes hard, spraying water. He turns around and looks at the bird; very damp, the wings and feet plastered down limp against the body. It lies in the beam of light coming down the alley.

Nepo peeks through a crack in the boxes, the lights of the truck flashing and backing down the alley towards him. He makes a tiny crying sound completely lost under the sound of the big truck. He looks around, he's at the end of the alley, and he cries. The light shines brighter and brighter on the bird's body. Nepo drops down into the blanket again, shaking and cold, the light and vibration of the truck getting closer.

He has his nose buried in the wet folds of the blanket as low as he can get it, but his eyes are open and alert, blinking and watching the light.

The big noise of the truck is almost on top of him now and he is shaking very hard. He keeps his eyes on the bird, the tiny pale yellow beak facing him.

Then he sees the truck.

It comes heavily and slowly and dripping black water and hissing with the huge roaring sound of the engine. A big rusty wheel rolls in front of Nepo. He looks at this and then back at the bird, and the distance between them. He looks at the beak and the tiny graceful crown of the head and the closed eyelids and he watches the bird disappear under the big black tire.

Nepo hears the small crunch of the bird under the tire and he buries his head lower into the blanket. He cannot close his eyes or stop shaking. The truck continues to back into the alley and the bird is gone.

The truck stops with a hiss, engine rumbling. Nepo hears the trash man get out of the cab of the truck and slam the door. He hears the man's boots stomping back from the truck, walking towards the stack of boxes. Nepo hears the man breathe and grunt as he takes the top boxes from the stack and flings them into the back of the truck. Each layer of boxes gone brings more light down onto Nepo, and he hunkers down in the freezing wet blanket.

For a moment Nepo doesn't hear the man anymore, no boxes move, nothing happens. Just the sound of the truck engine running. Then, behind him, a steamy liquid hits the wall and runs down to the blanket. The liquid steams off the wall. Now he hears the man grunt and breath and moan and make a kind of scratching sound, and then the boxes are taken away again until they're gone and Nepo sits alone and exposed on the blanket.

He looks up, very far up, and the trash man looks down at him.

The trash man stands very still in the rain, very tall from where the little dog looks up at him. His large head and body are a black silhouette against the grey-purple sky. And now he bends down to Nepo very slowly, his knees popping on the way down. He squats down close to Nepo, who doesn't move or make a sound. The man smells like the truck to Nepo, smoky and oily, and he can hear him breathing, but he can't see his face. And now the man's hand comes out of his jacket pocket and reaches over to Nepo's head. Nepo trembles badly and he lowers his head.

It's a long moment waiting for the hand to come down on him, and Nepo's eyes stay clenched shut, waiting.

The big dirty hand comes lightly down on the dog's wet head. The fingers come down around his skull and squeeze lightly. And now they begin to rub his head and ears, fluffing up the fur on his head, trying to dry it. The hand moves down to Nepo's shoulders, warming and drying, then down the back to the tail. The trash man can feel the dog trembling. He stands up and takes off his coat, walks back to the truck. Nepo watches as the man climbs up into the cab of the truck, light glowing out the door into the alley. In the cab, the trash man spreads his coat out on the seat, making a bed of the warm yellow wool lining. The man's grimy hand gently brushes the wool, fluffing it and trying to dry it as he had the dog's wet fur. He flicks a knob on the dashboard, turning up the heat, and points all the dash vents in the direction of the woolen bed. He climbs from the cab down into the alley.

Nepo has been listening and watching the shadows. He watches as the man comes back towards him. Nepo feels a hand slip under his soaked belly, the other holding his head, and he is lifted out of the wet blanket. Snug against the man's chest, he's held there a moment as the man strokes the furry shoulders and back. Nepo looks down at the blanket, and the feathers of the bird.

The trash man walks back to the truck, and Nepo is placed gently on the coat, his soaked and chilled paws touching the dry wool. He shakes off some of the wet, and stands in the blast of the truck heater, craning his head to the heat. He looks at the man, behind the steering wheel. He can just see him in the glow of the dashboard; thick and shaggy white-blonde hair messed up across a big round red face, two very large watery eyes looking into Nepo's eyes and smiling. The man looks at Nepo until the dog has to look away, and Nepo drops down into the woolen warm folds of the coat.

"Let's go home," the trash man whispers to the steering wheel, starting the truck down the alley towards the street.

Nepo rolls over onto his back letting the truck heater blow his belly dry and frizzy. Through the windows, he can see streetlights go by above the truck. He lies in the warmth and listens as the man drives.

Nepo is asleep when suddenly the truck stops. The man gets out of the truck and shuts the door. All is quiet, the truck motor turned off, the dashboard lights off. Nepo stands up in the dark and looks around, crying a little. He can't see anything through the windows but darkness. He looks and looks into the darkness but there's nothing there and he's scared. Then he hears footsteps.

The door opens and there he is, the trash man again!

Nepo's tail wags for the first time today. The trash man gets back behind the wheel with a great rustling of paper sacks and giggling and then there's a dog biscuit right in front of Nepo, who sniffs it and snatches it into his mouth. He chews and chews at the biscuit and licks his mouth and when he looks back to the trash man there's *another* biscuit! He takes this one too and as he chews away at it, he sees a pile of biscuits tossed onto the coat for him. His tail wags and as the man starts the truck, he feels the hot blast of the heater on him again, and he falls against the back of the seat as the truck lurches forward.

He looks up at the trash man who twists something open in a paper bag and drinks from it.

Giggling a little *more*, now.

Nepo is still working on the biscuits when the truck slows down and stops again. The trash man leans down smiling and laughing and talking to Nepo, then he jumps down out of the truck and shuts the door. The door on the other side of the truck opens and Nepo sees the front door of the shelter.

Sondra is standing there and like everyone else today, she's trembling.

And like a furry coiled-up spring, Nepo leaps out of the truck, scattering beef strips all over the cab, and lands in Sondra's arms.

In twenty minutes, Nepo and Sondra will be in bed, warm and peaceful.

In an hour or so, the trash man will also be in bed, *very* warm and peaceful.

IF YOU ARE IN A CERTAIN PUB TONIGHT in Cork, getting close to closing time, you'll see Rob, Tommy, and Declan, leaning on an old black piano. An old man has played the piano for hours, and moments ago he played his last note when he toppled forward exhausted and his head hit the keys. Tommy sings low to himself and drapes his jacket over the old man's shoulders. Declan listens to Rob, who is no longer silent and suspicious of him. Far from it, you can tell by the look on Rob's face.

Rob is writing and drawing on a piece of paper on the piano and talking very excitedly. Declan drinks and smiles at Tommy. Tommy nods at him, and goes on singing.

The old man looks up and thanks Tommy for the jacket, then takes it to the floor and lies down.

That's what you're watching, if you are in that certain pub tonight. Fast friends, planning something big.

While Rob goes on talking and writing and scheming ...

But if you happened to be at Kieran's Inn, you'd know that Kieran has bought a package of glazing for the loose bedroom window. Kieran brings the tube of glazing to the bedroom, Julie brings a bottle of wine, they sit on the edge of the bed to get ready for the work at hand, to get in the mood, and then they get in the mood for something else.

Hours later, they find the glazing and putty knife underneath her bra and Kieran's pants.

CHESTER LEAVES CORK

KIERAN SITS on the front step of the inn looking down the foggy road, waiting for Chester, who's late this morning. Kieran is not angry, but he is worried. He's been inside to refill his coffee twice already, and now he goes in for a third one, this one *half whiskey.*

Chester is at the bus station asking the price of a ticket to Dingle, one-way. And then he buys one. It's an hour until departure, so he walks across the street to a pub he's never been inside of before. He walks in, sees nobody he knows, and orders a pint of stout at the bar. After the foam has settled, he carries his pint to the fireplace at the back of the pub, and leans there, breathing in the peat fire smoke. He drinks long and deep because he wants to get in as many pints as he can in the next hour.

Rob walks up the hill to Chester's house. He's been trying to call him but Chester doesn't answer. The phone rings and rings. Rob wants to tell him the news. He had also called Kieran who told him Chester hasn't come to work yet. Hearing worry in Kieran's voice Rob hid his own, saying, "I'll find him!" He walks as fast as he can up the hill, but he's breathing hard and limping a bit.

As he makes the top of the hill he turns the corner, sees that the black gate to the front yard of Chester's house stands open, unlatched. It begins to rain now, and Rob splashes quickly up the street. He passes through the gate and crosses the yard, looks in the front room window. Lights are out, and everything is neatly in order, in place; neatly, orderly, and *unusually* in place. Chester's desk is cleared and empty. Rob tries the front door but it's locked so he knocks. Nothing inside, no sound.

Rob looks down the street towards town and the rain comes harder.

Kieran sits in the shuttle van, key in the ignition, staring out the windshield.

He's thinking how Chester was less cheerful yesterday, less talkative, less many things. Angry. And now Chester hasn't shown up for work. Last night Chester and Kieran had a talk and Chester had gotten drunk and started talking about turning fifty on Sunday. And that he had to make some kind of change before, or at least on, that birthday.

Kieran asked him what he meant by that.

"I feel that I've wasted time and now I'm running *out* of time, that everything I've done up to now has been a failure and I haven't reached my potential. I don't even know what it is. Maybe I'm not good at *anything*. When I think back—and this happens all the time in the middle of the night—I think back thirty years and I'm in college and I'm the same guy now that I was then, there have been no changes, I've wasted my life, and thirty years from now I'll be old or dead, one or the other. Probably."

Kieran waited for him to catch his breath and go on, but when Chester seemed to be finished and was staring at the floor, Kieran said something.

"Well, *that* was a lot of bullshit!"

Kieran was laughing when he said it but Chester got up and left.

Kieran sits in the van, key in the ignition, the engine silent.

Chester watches the foam settle on his third pint, checks the time and the bus station across the street—half an hour to go. The barman watches as Chester walks back to the fireplace in the back and faces the wall again. He wonders about Chester for a moment, then returns his attention to the soccer on the TV over the bar.

Rob walks slowly down the hill. He's completely wet now but in no hurry and not sure where to go or what to do next. He had been excited to tell Chester of Tommy's latest surprise concert, and of this new guy from out of town, Declan, who seems interested in promoting Tommy's singing career. As a partner, of course, a sort of junior partner to be sure, because Rob knows he's always known better than anyone what to do with Tommy, what the dream would be for him as a singer. But Rob has reluctantly welcomed this Declan man in (though he is secretly excited about it, and couldn't wait to tell Chester about it all).

But now, Chester isn't around and Rob doesn't understand this at all. And the excitement has gone out of the Tommy story, so Rob walks along slowly. Rob pulls his cap down lower because he's begun to cry. He hasn't cried in a long, long time.

On the bus, Chester watches people walking along Parnell Place as the bus backs out of the station. The sky has opened and sunshine comes down on the umbrellas and the wet heads. The people lower their umbrellas and shake off the wet, looking surprised and smiling and amused by the sudden sunlight. Chester stares out at them, then across the River Lee and up the hill to his house. He's bringing nothing from there. All he has is some money and the Dingle ticket.

The bus sweeps out of the station lot by the animal shelter and Chester looks over the fence to the dog yard. There's one little dog, sitting on his back legs, front legs braced wide in front, looking up at the sun.

And then the bus picks up speed through the Cork streets towards the edge of town and the countryside and Dingle.

MARY'S PERFECT TABLE

SUNLIGHT COMES through the tearoom window onto Mary's perfect table. She sits at her table, the Cork newspaper on her left, her teacup, teapot, and biscuit on her right, all lined up and perfect. She wishes she could draw so she could make a picture of this table, but then she decides it's enough to just *be* at this table this morning.

After just two days she has a routine. When she arrives at the tearoom the teapot is waiting at her table by the window, the table with her favorite view down Gill Abbey Street. And she takes her time, these mornings. She hasn't taken a sip of tea just yet, and the newspaper lies there fresh and crisp and she thinks about everything that's happened.

She thinks about how she has her regular table all to herself if she wants it, and they all say "Hello Mary" when she comes in. She thinks how just a few streets from here she has her manager job at the Rose Lodge. And over there, she has her manager office with a desk and a chair and a sitting area for visitors and employee interviews. She even hired an *assistant* manager! She has her own room upstairs, the same room she took when she arrived three days ago. She'll never want another one.

Mary takes a slow savoring sip of tea now and as she looks down Gill Abbey a bus crosses quickly and is gone. This gets her thinking about Kinsale and her wild decision to leave that place. And her other decision to leave her room and all her possessions behind, bringing almost nothing to Cork. Leaving her little collections and photograph albums and most of her clothes there in the room. And she smiles, thinking about that. Thinking about that and looking down at her perfect table.

"More hot water, Mary?" She looks up and young Ellen is there with a steaming pot, young beautiful Ellen, thinks Mary. Long black hair, green eyes, bright white waitress shirt and green wool sweater, always happy and always happy to see Mary.

"Yes, Ellen, thanks a million." It's all unofficial of course, but Ellen has become one of Mary's "daughters." Ellen officially seems to like it.

"So, how's the new boy comin' along at the lodge then? Workin' out, is he?"

Mary takes a bite of biscuit. She brushes some biscuit crumbs from her blouse, takes a sip of tea, smiling as she takes a little time with the answer, knowing how anticipated it is for Ellen.

"What's so funny, then?" Ellen knows why Mary is smiling, and why she's slow with the answer, but she's pretending to be mad. "Well?"

Mary looks out the window down Gill Abbey and sees the "new boy" coming down the street.

"Why not ask *him*?"

Ellen looks at Mary and then looks where she's looking and she sees Eric coming towards the tea room. Mary glances at Ellen.

"Oh, I have sausages burning, I ..." and Ellen is gone suddenly into the kitchen.

Mary watches Eric and remembers first seeing him on the bus from Kinsale, in the back of the bus, hiding behind a book. She recalls the night he had come in drunk with his broken glasses. And, of course, the time he'd been "excited" in the upstairs hallway of the lodge. And now here he comes, white shirt and red bow tie and black jacket and all that wild red hair slicked back neat on his head and carrying his new satchel.

He is equally in as much of a hurry as Mary is not, and here he comes into the tearoom.

"Morning Mary. Now the last thing I want to do is bother you in your free time, I'll be gone in a blink, but the egg delivery hasn't come through, we have a couple of dozen still, and I'm a bit worried about breakfast. I'm sure it'll all be alright, but I wanted to let you know." Eric lays his satchel on the table and picks it up again. "I mean, I'm sure there's to be no problem, we have two dozen eggs still, I wondered what you think. You know?"

Mary sips her tea. "How many guests do we have so far today, Eric?" Eric shifts his weight to his other foot and squints, looks out the window.

"Ehm, two couples, top floor. No reservations for tomorrow." He smiles at Mary. "Yeah, I see what you're drivin' at. OK, sorry, I'll leave you now. I'll get back to the lodge, sorry."

"Ellen? Can you come here please," Mary grins at Eric. "Love the new satchel, Eric. It suits you, you know." Mary turns and here comes Ellen, surprisingly fast.

"Yes, Mary? More hot water?" Ellen asks, looking at Eric. Mary looks back and forth at them, as they look at each other.

"No Ellen, I'm probably in enough hot water as it is." And now Ellen and Eric look at Mary.

"Ellen, I wanted you to meet my new assistant manager, Eric. Eric, Ellen."

That said, Mary takes another bite of biscuit. There's a strange fumbling handshake between them. A sort of mutual trembling. Big smiles though.

Mary looks at them after the handshakes are done. They stand there, not sure what to do next.

"What I am really curious to know is how you both get your shirts so white?" Mary laughs.

And again, they look at each other with no answer, but with one more thing in common now.

"Never mind. I wanted you two to meet. Ellen, can I have some sausages?" Ellen says yes to this by saying goodbye to Eric and starting back to the kitchen. But then she turns around and comes back. Mary notices that she nearly goes into a sort of curtsy and Eric nearly bows to her, neither of them really doing these things all the way, but almost, sort of. Then Ellen is gone and Eric has shifted his satchel to his other arm and is out the door suddenly, back down Gill Abbey towards the lodge. It all happens that fast.

And Mary smiles down at her perfect table.

THE DAWN OF TOMMY, INC.
(OR MAYBE TOMORROW)

DECLAN SITS in a pub waiting for Rob who is looking for Chester. He has his "Mission Statement" for Tommy in front of him on the table, and a pot of tea. He has some "Scenarios for Success" sketched out neatly and in a binder, ready for his meeting with Rob, who is now two hours late. And now Declan folds all these into his briefcase and latches it shut. He hasn't wanted to drink anything strong but he orders a vodka on ice and drinks it in one swallow. The barman gets the nod from Declan and pours another.

He begins to think of his father and how he hasn't had a phone call from him in all the days he's been in Cork. He's had the regular check come in the mail, but no calls, not even the tiny personal hand-written notes that used to come with the checks. His father doesn't know yet that Declan has given up on the business.

After watching Tommy sing in the street yesterday, Declan went back to his office. He hung speakers on the wall, on the same nails where his framed motivational slogans used to be. Also on the wall, he hung old album covers; records by the Pogues, Thin Lizzy, the Dubliners, Bob Dylan, his first copy of "Exile On Main Street," his first copy of "Rattle and Hum." A picture of the Beatles singing on a roof. Another picture of Sinead O'Connor tearing up a pope.

All of these things came out of a box he hadn't ever unpacked at the Holiday Inn.

Still, he wonders why he hasn't heard from his father. And sitting in the pub waiting for Rob, who hasn't shown up yet, he thinks he'd better leave. He thinks maybe Rob isn't coming. The excitement of yesterday begins to fade away. I've done it again, he thinks.

He swallows the second vodka and the barman is on his way already with number three.

Declan wants to get away, out of the pub, maybe out of Cork, but where next? He had believed in coming to Cork for a brand new start where nobody knows him, but now he's thinking he's made a fool of himself somehow with this singer and his business partner, who he's sure aren't coming now. And he's thinking that this barman even knows about that, that he's feeling sorry for Declan now, and counting how many vodkas he's already had.

This being Cork, the barman isn't counting anyone's drinks. He sets a new drink on the table in front of Declan.

"Here's one on me, sir."

Declan stares at the new vodka in front of him. He has never been called sir in his life. Not that he can remember at this moment. The barman goes back behind the bar. When he gets there Declan picks up his vodka to toast him and the barman raises his ongoing glass of wine, saying, "He'll be here."

And with that, he is.

Rob stands in the pub door, shaking off the rain, smiling at Declan, who's looking over at the barman, who is stunned by his own sense of timing.

The little cluster of men at the end of the bar watch this wordless back and forth between Rob and the barman and Declan and break out laughing and coughing. One of them calls out.

"Don't be shy, gents. Do ye need an introduction then?" More wheezing laughter and pounding on the bar from these men now, as Rob and Declan focus on each other in the dark pub. Rob walks slowly into the room, into the yellow light, and the men can see his red eyes, and that he's been crying.

They start coughing again and suddenly they are talking loudly about soccer.

Rob comes to Declan's table and stands a moment before he sits down.

"I am sorry Declan," he says to the tabletop. "I was looking for a friend who is just gone I guess. Chester. I don't know, something's wrong, something's really wrong I think ... "He traces a drink ring on the tabletop round and round with a finger and finally looks at Declan, who is very uneasy with this, though he's stopped thinking about his father and his own life. He doesn't want to hide or go home now, but he's not used to someone coming to him upset and apologizing.

Like he's not used to someone calling him sir.

Over at the bar, the one who made the joke about introductions watches the table as his friends go on talking and coughing and laughing and—one of them—*burping*, as loudly as he can. The one watching the table motions the barman over with a secret, conspiratorial wink, and lays down some euros on the bar.

"What are you drinkin', Rob?" The barman pours another vodka and waits for Rob's drink order. Rob twists in his chair towards the bar, thankful for the question, thankful to break away from the awkward silence at his table. "Oh, a cider, yes, thanks ever so much, a cider," and when Rob sees the barman nod towards the man at the end of the bar, he goes on. "And you're buyin' then, are you? Well, thanks very much. Thanks very much indeed." Rob stays twisted in his seat towards the bar, smiling and laughing and thanking everybody over there again until the drinks are poured and on the way, not sure how to talk to Declan. Not wanting him mad at him for being late. Not wanting to think about where Chester is. Not wanting to start crying again.

Declan breaks the silence.

"Um, Chester is his name, your friend?"

The drinks come and Rob grabs the cider, hiding his face.

"I can see you're worried about him, Rob, and it's ok you're late, I mean I was going over some papers, you know, I wrote some things down about Tommy, and I was looking over that before you came in, so, you know, I wasn't even noticing the time, I mean, not really." This all comes out fast and they both take long sips of their drinks.

Rob looks at the briefcase on the table.

"You've already been working on this?"

Declan unlatches his briefcase and pulls out his notes, lays them out in front of Rob whose red eyes get really big as he picks up a piece of paper.

"Strategies for success. You wrote this, Declan?"

Rob reads down the page slowly. The writing is very thick with business words and phrases, Rob thinks, but every time he sees his name and Tommy's in bold capital letters, he's excited. In fact, Rob is getting very excited about what he's reading, though he doesn't understand a lot of it. He had been worried that Declan would be pushing him out and away from being involved with Tommy's singing career, but as he continues reading, his name showing up again and again in every paragraph, he knows he's wrong. Declan is just doing what he and Tommy cannot do. And at the bottom of the page, there's a phrase that he really likes.

"ROB will at all times be the lead spokesman and key advertising liaison for TOMMY with regards to all face-to-face conversations and other forms of oral communications with all venues, be they—universities, pubs, churches, music halls, auditoriums, and stadiums. The aforementioned applies in Ireland, the U.K., and throughout the E.U."

Rob feels tears coming again, and after a quick look into Declan's eyes, he turns away to the bar, looking for the barman, who is on the floor with a towel. The man in the cluster of men at the bar who has been repeatedly burping has now thrown up all over the bar and one of his friends and the floor, and now creeps to the toilet muttering to himself. His friends and even the barman laughs as he creeps away. The barman elbows one of the others on the floor, "Bit earlier than usual, eh Donal?" And they laugh again, all getting down on the floor with towels.

Rob looks back to Declan and they both start laughing.

When the laughter has slowed down and stopped and the floor has been mopped up, the barman brings another round and Declan asks Rob if the contract is ok.

"Where do I sign?" says Rob.

"Oh, no, no signing, nothing *that* formal. Here—let's drink a toast instead. And next, we'll show it to Tommy."

Rob clinks glasses with Declan and drinks his drink. He's smiling and studying Declan.

"What?" asks Declan.

"Are you in the music business? I mean, it's alright if you aren't, I was just wondering. Do you have an office somewhere?"

Declan thinks about his office. All that new office equipment sitting there in a dark room. Record albums and speakers on the walls.

"Yes, there's an office," he says, drinking his drink. Proud for once. Even if everything is soon gone and he's kicked out of the building, there will still be an office; maybe his apartment, maybe this bar, this table, but somewhere. Rob smiles.

"What did you do in Killarney, Declan? Is that where you said you were from?"

"I'm from Dublin. I tried to work at my father's business but after awhile he got me a job at the Holiday Inn in Killarney as a manager. But the time came when I wanted my own investment consulting business so I came here and opened an office. My father paid for all of that of course, not much money in managing the Holiday Inn as you might imagine. He still sends me money, you know, until I get the business off the ground. He's been loads of help to me, *you know?*"

Rob *doesn't* know what to make of this. He believes the story but doesn't believe Declan will get his investment consulting business off the ground. Or even wants to. It doesn't make him trust him less, though. He certainly doesn't

like him less. He still wants to be partners with him, that
hasn't changed. And somehow he doesn't buy the thing
Declan has said about his father being loads of help.

"That's grand, Declan. Well, uh, is your father still in
Dublin?"

"Yes, his offices are right on the River Liffey. He's very
successful. Everyone knows him in Dublin."

Rob believes *this* is true and it inspires another question.

"When did you last see him?"

"Oh ages ago care for another cider Rob?"

Declan says this quickly and is up from the table and on
his way to the bar, stumbling into a chair along the way. Rob
smiles faintly, looking down at the tabletop again.

"That I would, Declan, that I would. Let's get drunk and
toast all our loving families. And Chester, wherever he is.
We'll start the business tomorrow."

LET GO, LOCK THE DOOR

KIERAN'S INN IS EMPTY and Kieran is still sitting in the van, staring out the windshield. Julie watches him from the kitchen window. She's just up from sleeping late and her long brown hair falls down across her face, leaving one bleary eye to watch Kieran. She is naked and waiting for her tea kettle to get hot.

She has gotten out of bed ready for sex. A lot more sex, sex like last night. She woke up, smelled last night in the sheets and on her hands, and rolled over open for Kieran. Now downstairs, she watches him outside, thinking either he's wanting to do it again in the van this time or that something's going on, something's happened, something's wrong.

Still, she's ready for more of last night. As she watches him through the window, she touches her nipples. She's alone in the kitchen, the kitchen usually filled with at least ten or more guests behind her at the table. She pivots around on her toes and stretches out one leg onto that table and softly touches herself, her sharp inhaling mixed with slow breathing.

The tea kettle is also steaming now and she takes a large overripe strawberry from the fruit basket, which now smells like her and Kieran, and pops it into her mouth. Slowly, like a ballerina, she lifts her leg from the table, and bows to the table as if there were an entire guest register of customers sitting there. "Good morning," she says, pours a cup of tea, wraps a blanket around herself and goes outside to Kieran.

Kieran watches Julie walk towards him in the rearview mirror. She's smiling and just barely holding a blanket around herself, and her feet are getting muddy. He gets out of the van, gladly breaking free of his thoughts. He stands and smiles and waits for her, opens his arms and takes her in, feeling those nipples even through the blanket.

"Oh yeah?" he says with a laugh, "Oh *really*?"

Julie hugs him, slides a hand inside his robe and grabs him, and he is cold, cold, cold.

"How long have you been out here?" she asks. "I have some strawberries inside that'll really warm you up. That's a double entendre, by the way." He doesn't laugh at this much. She looks up at him and takes his hand.

"Let's get back in, honey."

In the van, he slides back down behind the wheel and Julie drops down into the passenger seat, pulling the blanket around her and planting her bare feet against the windshield. Kieran is lost in thought again, wondering about Chester, but not so lost in thought that he doesn't see those toes spread on the glass, and his grin comes back.

"You know Julie, I must say I love those feet of yours." Kieran's eyes follow Julie's legs into the blanket wrapped around her. He slips it open at her breasts.

"And I love these. I forget sometimes what happens to you when one goes into my mouth."

Julie reaches up and locks her door. "I never forget," she says.

Kieran reaches over and locks his door.

A little while later Julie nearly pushes that windshield right out of the van.

WAIT UNTIL THEY GET TO KNOW YOU

FOG HAS SWALLOWED up the countryside outside as Chester's bus heads west.

The cold and rain out there and the heat inside have fogged the windows so Chester tries to read the ugly slashing graffiti on the back of the seat in front of him. Black and red marks that make no sense to him as he stares at them and feels like a fugitive. He looks over at the noisy teens across the aisle. One boy has no front teeth and lots of big red pimples and he drinks a can of grape soda almost in a gulp, then opens a cola can. He is wired and also wired into a headset but the music can be heard everywhere in the bus as he reads a movie and music magazine and chews away at a chocolate bar.

None of this is exactly Chester's Irish traveling fantasy and the fact that he has to piss very badly is also unromantic, to say the least.

Chester looks back out the window but sees himself in the glass. He's been avoiding mirrors lately but there he is and the face frightens him.

He takes out his unread *Irish Times* and pages through it until he finds a full-page advert with lots of white space above a cruise ship and he begins making a list there.

    1) That last phone call they said you'd never
        change and then of course they cried.
        Before they yelled.

    2) That this "Irish Thing" is just the latest
        example of how lost I am.

3) You are still writing notes about them and you're almost 50.

4) You're still thinking about them and you're almost 50.

5) I left my house in Cork and the sweet landlady doesn't even know I'm gone.

6) I left my job with Kieran. I didn't tell him.

7) I didn't say goodbye to Rob. Or to Kieran or Tommy.

8) I don't know what I'm doing.

9) Why didn't I tell anybody anything? They're friends.

10) I'm just like this kid across the aisle.

Chester looks over at the boy with the chocolate and headset, scratches out number ten, but adds an eleven.

11) Running again. They WERE my friends there in Cork. But then dad said that thing again about wait until they get to know you like WE do.

12) (Then I broke the phone.)

He folds the newspaper in half and lays it on the empty seat by him. Out the window, a sign for Tralee comes clear as it comes near and passes by. Just a few more kilometers, just a few more minutes. The sun breaks out again and lights up the town ahead and the surrounding green hills. To kill time until the bus depot and not think about having to piss, he begins counting the sheep all over the hills. The moving white spots in the distance and the hay-chewing faces right at the roadside. He counts fifty-six sheep before the bus slows and turns into the Tralee station. Chester picks up the newspaper, gets off the bus, and looks right away for the bathroom.

After peeing, he reads the schedule and finds he has over an hour before the connecting bus for Dingle arrives, so he walks down into town. A couple of streets later he finds a pub and walks inside to a large, warm, softly lit room. A short, black-vested man with a red face and wild blonde hair walks across the room immediately with his hand out. Chester notices the man's energy and thinks it's as if his face is on fire and the wild hair is the smoke …

"Welcome to Kirby's, sir! Sit anywhere you like. Will you be eating then? Are you just off the bus? Our carvery table is open over there, all you can eat, or we have the menu as well. But have a seat anywhere you like, can I get you a drink to begin with?" Chester has been shaking hands with the little man through this entire welcome.

"Yes, a Black and Tan please," he says, continuing to shake the man's hand.

"A Black and Tan, very good, my name's John, and yours?" Chester tells him and then the man is off to the bar, walking like a very cheerful and energetic red-haired penguin.

When he comes back with the drink he sets it in front of Chester with a short bow and asks again, "Is it to be the carvery then?" Chester tells him he's leaving in an hour on the Dingle bus, and asks if he'll have the time.

"Oh aye, come with me, we'll speed this all right along."

John leads Chester to the carvery table where three young men in white jackets and tall chef's hats step forward together. In a flash, his plate is full; slices of turkey, mashed potatoes, carrots, biscuits, sausages, green beans, gravy over all, fish and chips, and so much steam rising off the plate into his glasses that John has to lead Chester back to his table.

"Where are you off to, Chester, if you don't mind me asking?"

"Dingle. I'm coming from Cork. America before that. This is a one-way trip."

This slows John down a moment, then he's smiling again.

"Sláinte!" he says, and walks back to the bar where a television set blinks across the bar, loud voices coming out of speakers behind the bottles.

John watches the TV with the bartender and the three cooks. The screen is split in two, American and British politicians talking about the war in the ancient desert.

John kicks the bar rail which startles everyone.

"Sorry, lads. But it's old news. It's the same. It's the same again and again. These old fucks think that if you keep killing it'll kill all the killing. Enough killing will kill killing and bring peace. It's the same all the time. Please turn that shit off." The bartender and the cooks smile at each other as John straightens up and tightens his tie, pulls down his vest, and turns back to the dining room.

And the big smile is there again. He's on the move.

In a corner of the pub, a thin old woman wrestles with her bags under the table containing who knows what, and jiggles her cup of tea from which she still hasn't drunk a drop. She jiggles and wrestles and shifts around in her chair. John walks over and sits down across from her at her table, talking to her softly. He reaches across the table and takes a sip from her cup. He makes a face.

"Oh, cold isn't it? I'll be right back." He takes the teapot from the table and he's off to the bar for fresh hot water. He comes back and pours for her. She takes a sip and now she smiles for the first time. "Oh that's fine, yes, thanks very much," she says. John squeezes her hand and is on his feet again, looking around.

He walks back towards the bar where the television set still flickers, this time about celebrities giving tours of their multiple homes, and John gets up on a bar stool and punches it off. Now the pub is quiet. It's just the music from the Tralee radio station. John looks back at Chester and smiles, then walks down a hallway and disappears around a corner.

Chester finishes lunch, pushes his plate across the table and looks at his watch. Plenty of time. He puts *The Irish Times* to the side and just sits. Plenty of time to just sit. He closes his eyes and faintly hears the music and the low, friendly talking from a table across the room. He hears rain on the windows, but it's warm in the pub. He thinks about maybe accidentally missing the bus. And he falls asleep.

"Looks as though we have still twenty-five minutes to departure!"

John is suddenly back, his hand on Chester's shoulder, and Chester wakes back up. "Anything else then, lad?"

Chester asks if there are any cigars for sale. John salutes and winks and walks back behind the bar where he pulls drawers out, opens cabinets, at last finds a wooden box and pulls out a thick cigar. He rolls it on the bar, sniffs it, then raises it in the air, smiling and winking again at Chester.

After all that, Chester wonders if he can afford it.

John comes back and places it in front of Chester along with a box of matches.

"This is for you, Chester, compliments of Kirby's Inn."

John sticks his hand out for Chester to shake. Chester shakes hands and thanks him. John puts the bill on the table, starts away from the table, turns back.

"None of my business but don't dangle out in Dingle. That's a kind of joke, but it's what somebody once told me. Then, of course, I stayed out there too long anyway and wound up back here in Tralee, not so far away. Take care, lad. Be glad to see you again should you return this way. Goodbye." This time John crosses the bar and goes into the kitchen.

Chester looks down at the cigar and the check. Underneath the check, there's a note written in big looping strokes and long slashes crossing the t's, finished by several bold exclamation points.

Chester sits and stares at the note. He turns his head a bit to the side, away from the tables on the other side of the pub.

The note doesn't make sense to Chester, it almost makes him laugh. It doesn't make sense to him that this man would write a note like this when he's only been here an hour.

Chester looks around for John but he's gone somewhere in the back. The old lady sips her tea and the cook and the barman have the TV back on, watching soccer. He'd felt that one of them would be watching him, but they're all busy.

He reads the note again. Then he looks down into his wallet and pulls out too many euros for the tab, picks up the cigar and the note and stands up. The cook and the barman notice Chester leaving and each hold up a hand goodbye. Chester waves back smiling at them and is out the door.

It's colder outside now, raining hard. Chester keeps his eyes down and walks quickly towards the bus depot, and he's crying. He makes a sound that he hasn't heard come out of himself since he was a child, and he keeps making the sound to try and get it out of him before he boards the bus. He hopes the bus is empty, just him and the driver, but as he turns the corner, there is a small crowd gathering at the depot.

The bus is full and noisy with laughter and conversation. The driver is entertaining the people in the first rows with loud, slightly dirty jokes. He has given his bus driver hat to a little girl who wears it low over her eyes and staggers up and down the aisle showing it to everyone. Chester is towards the back again in a window seat. As the bus slowly winds through Tralee, Chester looks down the street to where Kirby's Pub is, gets a glimpse of it, and then it's gone.

The bus disappears west, into the fog.

In the pub, John sits where Chester sat and reads *The Irish Times*. He comes to the full-page advert of the cruise ship and Chester's list. The bartender watches John's face.

"So Johnny, what's in the paper today?"

John doesn't answer for a moment. Then he puts the paper down on the table and looks at the door where Chester went out.

"Just life, lad."

WHAT'S AFOOT WITH CHESTER?

THE WINDSHIELD of the Kieran's Inn Shuttle Van is not broken out but it is very fogged up as Kieran and Julie sleep under a blanket in the back.

Rob and Declan circle around the van.

"I can't see but I don't think there's anyone in there, Declan. Funny thing, though, that the inn is open and no one at home but this van is locked. What do you think it all means?" Declan leans in closer, rubbing the glass on the passenger side of the van and there's a bare foot resting on top of the seat inside.

"Rob, I see a foot."

Rob comes over and shoulder to shoulder with Declan, they look at the foot.

"I hope it's not a dead foot," says Declan.

They go on looking in silence.

"I don't know your friend Chester, but do you think it's his foot?"

"*No*—this is a *feminine* foot."

Declan looks again but he can't make that distinction at all through the foggy glass.

"How can you say for sure? I see no polish on the toenails."

"Well Declan, I *will* say that I've known men who painted their nails, all of twenty of 'em. That's another story but, no, this is a woman's foot. It's sexy. You know, our feet—men's feet?—well, I always hide mine, I don't know about you. The last thing that comes off at night are my socks, and that's in the dark. When it comes to feet, women spend more time on their feet than we do when it comes to the beauty routine."

They go on staring at the dead or alive but *female* foot.

In the back of the van, Kieran opens his eyes slowly, looking around and trying to remember where he is, then smiles and yawns feeling Julie's hand between his legs. Her head - smelling like strawberries, from her skin cream he assumes - is on his chest and he leans down and kisses her ear, sucking on the lobe. This snaps her awake and her foot flies off the front seat. Rob and Declan, both startled, bump their heads on the window and jump back from the van.

"What the fuck was that?" Kieran whispers, squinting through the foggy windows. Julie sits up and squeezes her breasts back inside her robe, and looks where Kieran is looking.

"Good thing we locked the doors, Kieran. HELLO?" Silence outside. Julie looks at Kieran and shrugs as he pulls himself back into his pants and zips up.

He tries now. "HELLO? Can we help you?"

The two dark figures in the foggy glass move a little closer towards the car. It's quiet for a moment.

"Kieran? Is that you inside? And Julie, is that you in there as well? It's Rob. I wondered if you'd heard from Chester. Declan drove me out here to see if there was any news of him. Oh, you don't know Declan, do you? Allow me to introduce my new friend Declan from Killarney. Well, in truth, he's from Dublin, but he was in Killarney in the hospitality trade like yourselves but he has come to Cork now to make a fresh start. Not necessarily anymore in the hospitality trade. Maybe, maybe not. A new start. I can relate to that, can't you? Looking for a new start?"

Rob has finished and leans forward towards the van, listening. Declan looks at him, shaking his head a little and smiling. He puts a hand on Rob's shoulder and thanks him for the detailed introduction. Rob nods, concentrating on any sound that might be coming from inside.

What he hears is Kieran and Julie laughing wildly.

A few moments later Kieran sits down next to Rob at the kitchen table.

"Not a word, Rob. I've no idea where he is."

Julie sits grinning across the table still in her robe, steam drifting up from the teapot in front of her. She watches Rob and her husband, both of them very worried. She looks over at Declan, sitting a bit off to the side of the table by himself. Kieran listens to Rob's ideas of where Chester might be but he's looking at Declan, and he leans towards him. "Declan? Drink?"

"Well, you know yes ... oh well, maybe not. I'll just have tea," he says, smiling at Julie.

Kieran looks at Rob. "I know *you're* not drinking tea. How about it? Your usual *vin rouge*?" Rob perks up and stops talking about Chester for a moment.

"Kieran, that would be just grand. And Declan here is a vodka man. Vodka man from way back, eh, Declan?"

"Vodka man. That I am!" Declan says this like he's just realized it. He has perked up suddenly too, and he realizes he's just winked at everybody. He can't remember ever winking at anyone but himself in the mirror, practicing to be that kind of man. Maybe he is that kind of man. He leans back in his chair, crosses his legs, nearly loses his balance, and waves an arm in the air. "From way back!"

Kieran slams the tabletop. "Vodka it is!" And he's up and over to the bar. Julie grins and rolls her eyes, swinging her bare feet up onto the table in the middle of the men. "Does everyone in Cork drink, for fuck sake?" She's laughing with the question though, not really asking.

Kieran, also laughing, answers from the bar. "Oh yes, Julie. Most of us, dear." He comes back to the table, sets the drinks before Rob and Declan, and kisses Julie's wiggling toes.

Then he pours the tea for her.

A PIGEON WINKS AT TOMMY
AND SONDRA LETS HIM IN

TOMMY WALKS along the river, along Merchant's Quay, and he comes alongside the bus station. It's a beautiful day with a very high blue sky, bright white clouds sailing over very fast, and the quick wind carries the strong fishy sea smell. Pigeons are flying crazily in all directions and they can be heard talking in the wind above. People are walking along laughing and holding onto whatever is on their heads, the wind is so strong. Tommy stops and leans on a bridge railing and watches one small little rolling cloud. He marks it over a building across the river and then he turns around and finds the Cork animal shelter and looks there for as long as he can, even holding his breath. When he turns back around to the building across the water the little rolling cloud has rolled on to the top of another batch of buildings down the river.

Above, a pigeon breaks off from a flock of other birds and glides down softly onto the river where it folds its wings in and settles, floating along on the choppy water. Tommy watches this bird for a long time as it floats along with the strong tide until it's out of sight under the bridge. At the last moment, before the little bird is gone under the bridge, the pigeon cocks its head to the side, looks up, and aims a tiny black eye right up at Tommy.

Later, he would say that the bird had winked at him, and that had given him the courage.

Because now Tommy straightens up from the bridge railing, pulls his cap down low so he doesn't lose it to the wind but also because he likes how it makes him look, and walks back to the crosswalk leading to the animal shelter across the street. He waits for the light to change.

The wild wind and the sea smell and the happy, free chaos of everything and everyone blowing around into each other on the street, the river full of waves and spray, and of course, the winking bird; all of it makes him feel ecstatically hopeful and joyful.

The light goes green.

As Tommy crosses the street with the shelter ahead in his eyes getting nearer he can feel his nerves rippling down his arms and fingers and his heart speeding up but not, this time, his second-guessing brain kicking in, like usual. Like normal. He keeps on walking and when he gets to the shelter door and knocks he has knocked without seeing the closed sign. And he knocks again.

He hears dogs barking inside and when the door opens Sondra is standing there in a Beamish Stout t-shirt and red rubber boots up to her bare knees. Nepo stands behind her in the vestibule with his front legs spread but he's not barking. Sondra smiles and leans against the door frame, a hand on her hip.

"Hello there, Tommy. Mister Songbird of Cork." With the hand on her hip, she flips her hair behind her shoulder and then the hand goes back to the hip. She smiles a little bigger and waits. Tommy smiles too and looks down the street. Nepo drops to the floor and falls asleep.

"Songbird. You saw the handbills."

"I did, Tommy. You are, you know."

"Yeah?"

"Yeah. Tommy, did you need something?" Sondra smiling even a little bit bigger now.

"Yes. Do you?"

Tommy looks at her and she doesn't look away.

"I do."

Sondra takes his hand, pulls him through the front door and her tongue is in his mouth, her eyes open, looking into his. Tommy likes this. He kisses her right back. Holding her, he slides a hand down her back past the bottom of her t-shirt to skin. The kiss goes on and on and he feels her hand on the back of his neck. Her other hand is like a butterfly flitting around his zipper.

When the kiss ends and they're both breathing like they've been running, Tommy says, "Wow." Sondra shuts the door, and with her butterfly hand she pulls Tommy towards the bedroom.

"Right, Tommy. Wow. Now, say that word backwards ... and come with me."

And outside the wind blows and the clouds roll and the pigeon floats on down the river, winking up at anyone else who needs him to.

DON'T THINK ALONE

CHESTER PACES in the dim yellow overhead light of his bed and breakfast room in Dingle with the sound of water gushing out of a faucet. He fills the bathtub with cold water. A case of beer and two bottles of white wine will go into the tub to chill for the long night ahead.

The water isn't so cold really but he knows that won't matter later, after the lubrication of the pubs. Warm or cold, he'll get the alcohol into his blood and brain, and the goal is to do that as fast as he can.

He paces back and forth in the little room. He walks across the narrow width of the room, from the door to the window, and counts four steps. At the window, he looks out into the night coming down dark blue and faintly sees the water splashing in the harbor and the boats with their lights on. Next, he paces the length of the room and it's ten steps from the bathroom door to the bed. He looks at a small framed painting over the bed. It's a grey stone house with a yellow thatched roof on a green field and a black dog and nothing else. The sky in the painting is the unpainted canvas. Must have been a cloudy day. It's signed by the artist, the same name as the man working the front desk downstairs. The front desk, which is also the end of a long, busy bar.

He turns off the cold faucet and starts putting the bottles into the bathtub water.

Chester lies down on the bed for a moment but is out of it and up again as if a fire bell had gone off, and he's pacing again. He hears people coming down the hall and freezes. The people go by jingling keys, pass his door, and he wonders why he froze. He tries to remember the last conversation he had with someone he knows but stops and opens the first beer. He drinks as much as he can right away. The first bottle takes a couple of minutes and he's into another one. He's feeling better now and as he paces back and forth he starts to philosophize about his drinking progression.

Right now, he is in the happy, free, "old friend" part—the beer being his old friend. This is the expansive part of the night, and he feels good, worries getting farther away from him. He is taking only ten paces back and forth lengthwise and only four across the middle, but he is in Ireland! Out on the Dingle Peninsula, in Dingle! Far from home, away from Cork, on his own. Anything is possible and he opens a third beer.

The next section is the "fuck-everybody-else-they-don't-understand-me" section, and he knows he's moving into it quickly. As he paces back towards the bathroom side of the room, he opens another beer from the tub and now he's pacing with two bottles, which he doesn't realize at first, but then he laughs, holds them up and clinks them together, toasting himself. He hears more people in the hall going by his door and toasts them too. Hearing people in the halls of this inn gets him to thinking about Kieran's Inn and Kieran and Julie, his job there, his friends there, but he drinks the thought of that away with the toast—*They don't understand me either*.

Chester pees in the toilet and as he stands there, he counts the bottles in the bathtub. He looks in the mirror over the toilet and his hair is sticking up like the thatched roof in the painting. His eyes are open wide and he's forcing a strange smile. And now he is not so sure about going out of the room. He knows he is soon to be into the third stage of his drinking routine. In this stage, he thinks that there's something very wrong with him. In this stage, anything is possible, and usually bleak. Eventually, in this stage, he starts thinking that *everything* is wrong with him, and then there's not enough to drink anywhere.

But he's not in this stage yet. He tries to think himself back into the first expansive stage, into that feeling. He knows if he stays in the room any longer, he won't leave. He zips up, splashes cold water on his face, and smooths down his thatched roof. He breaks out of the mirror trance, out of the bathroom, and gets ready to go out into Dingle; coat, key, hat.

But he lingers now, walking around the room, looking at everything, making sure it will be a warm, safe, temporary home for later when he comes back and will really need this room to be a temporary home, or a hiding place. He turns the bedside lamp down to its lowest glow, smooths the bedspread, opens the door and shuts it. Still inside the room.

After a long moment leaning against the door, Chester walks over to the painting over the bed and looks at it again. He likes this little piece of art, this little crude creation. The old guy downstairs somehow one day made this, maybe between pouring pints or checking in the guests. He probably didn't even think twice, he just did it.

Chester thinks *he did this painting without worry, probably*. He thinks *he painted this freely and nobody was over the shoulder saying anything, I hope*. He thinks *he made this painting and put it in a frame and hung it in this room and he's proud of it, I can tell*.

What a way to be, he thinks, and leaves the room.

In the pub downstairs, Chester orders a pint then sits away from the bar. He writes on bar napkins while he waits for the pint. He's describing the people at the bar and maybe he'll go talk to them after he's done. The pint comes and he spills a bit of it on his notes and the ink blurs into blue blobs, so he crumples them up in a wet ball. There's a basket of chips on the table and he eats all of them. He is getting sick and feels that he needs to empty himself out in every way possible, and maybe go back upstairs and go to bed. But he watches the people at the bar. One of them walks over to him, an old man and bent over some. The man focuses sharply on Chester, leans down into him with his eyes, and sits down with him.

"You're a bit messed up, aren't you? You're real drunk, aren't you? What's your name anyway?"

"Chester."

"Chester. I mean, it's ok, that's my wife over there, can you see her? If you can, then you're probably still not too drunk, so come on, you can join us, but listen ... "

Chester gets up and gets out of the pub, gets outside into the cold and walks along the harbor for awhile. He's wet and dizzy and lost but he finds the street guided by the light and music of another pub.

There's loud music in this pub and he yells his order for a pint over the singing. There are couples dancing near the band and families and children sitting together at tables. He stares at the couples dancing and the families but doesn't write about them. He finishes the pint and orders another with a shot of whiskey and writes on the new bar napkin.

He writes in big letters, tearing the napkin a little—

WHAT'S WRONG WITH ME?

The barman brings the pint and the whiskey, tosses out paper coasters to put them on, but stops, cranes his neck down and reads Chester's napkin. He looks down at Chester.

"Probably nothin' lad," he shrugs, puts Chester's drinks down, and walks to the Guinness tap.

The barman is drawing a pint when he looks back at Chester, points to his own head, and makes a circular motion with his finger.

"All in your head, man. Isn't that why you're here?" He waves at the rest of the pub. "Why *they're* here?" He turns back to the pint he's pouring, shuts off the tap, leaves the blonde head to settle down, and points at Chester.

"Think about it. But don't think too long," he says and laughs. "And don't think alone. Drink alone maybe, sure, sometimes. Or maybe not. But thinking alone, no, not too long anyway. Cheers." And then the barman is gone, into the kitchen.

Chester is drunk but not *that* drunk. He hears this.

He begins to think about it but smiles and stops and turns around and looks at the pub. The dancers dancing and the band playing. Everyone, families and friends and strangers, all sitting around the pub together. He leaves money on the bar and walks out of the pub and still hears the music a block away walking back towards his bed and breakfast.

And he's really staggering but he's being careful because he knows he's staggering. He also feels on solid ground for the first time in a long ... maybe the first time.

It's a narrow, broken sidewalk he's walking and there are footsteps coming towards him with no streetlights overhead, so it's dark and he's trying to be careful not to run into anybody, and he thinks, for a moment, that he'll walk out to the harbor and look at the water, stand out there on the dock for awhile and figure things out, but he keeps on towards the B and B because walking out to look at the water alone means he'll be thinking and thinking and thinking alone and it's what he always does.

His mind is whirling non-stop like this now, but he keeps walking.

He walks for awhile, he walks the streets of Dingle. He keeps walking and staggering, looking in the windows. Chester is very wet and cold and he's worried the B and B will be closed and dark, but when it comes into sight ahead there are lights on inside. In another minute he's in there, shaking off the rain and rubbing his hands together and though he can't remember ordering the pint it's being handed to him by the barman, front desk man, and painter.

"Thanks. I like that painting in my room. You made it?"

"Thanks. Yeah, that's mine. I'm pretty good."

"You are good. Hey, so is this beer. What is it?"

"That's Smithwick's. It's a nice change of pace from the heavier stouts."

Chester takes another drink and says, "Yes, that's true."

The old man who came to Chester earlier is sitting next to Chester with his wife. He elbows Chester.

"You should see the painting in my room. It's of *me!* It's a portrait he did last time we were here. It's me from the side, in profile. I look good in it. Better than real life, maybe." The man's wife, the barman, and Chester all wave at him that he's wrong about that.

The barman points to a painting behind the bar. It's of a very peaceful-looking dog lying on the floor with its eyes closed.

"That's my darling Sonia. Sweetest animal I ever knew."

They all look at the painting in silence, smiling. The old man next to Chester laughs.

"She looks so peaceful. Like she's sleeping the sleep of the dead."

"She was," says the bartender. "This was painted just before I buried her."

Everybody's quiet again. Chester takes a drink and decides to change the subject.

"You know what someone said to me tonight? He told me —*don't think alone.*"

The bartender stares at Chester, then pours himself a short beer and takes a drink. He looks at Chester again.

"Are you sure that he didn't say don't *drink—*"

"No, that's what I thought too, but he said don't *think* alone."

They all sit there and think about that. The old man's wife picks up her glass.

"I like that. And I'll drink to it."

The barman begins to count the cash drawer, so Chester and the old couple start up the stairs. The barman says good night and asks if they all have enough blankets for the night.

They all say yes though none of them remember their bedding situation at the moment. But it's a nice question.

They come to Chester's room first. The little round old woman gives Chester a tight, lasting hug and her perfume stays right on him after she lets go. She backs away and beams up at him. Her husband has a heavy white eyebrow line like a hawk and one eye goes off in a different direction and he doesn't smile but his voice is friendly and soft. He shakes Chester's hand and is clearly warming up to ask a question. He looks at his wife, looks down the hall, down at his feet, coughs, then asks it.

"Where are you from, Chester?"

"Cork."

"Good place. Good people. When do you go home?"

"Tomorrow."

"Fair play. Well. Sorry about before. Downstairs. I saw you over there, getting so drunk and I wondered about you. Worried about you. Good night, Chester. See you in the morning."

The old man coughs again and walks down the hall, his wife hugs Chester again then follows her husband down to their door and now the entire hallway smells of her perfume. Before they go into their room, they both look back to Chester and wave. The woman blows him a kiss.

Chester goes into his room and the bedside lamp he's left on for coziness is orbiting the bed like a moth, round and round and round. Chester walks uphill towards the side of the room that's rising and when he gets there he runs into the wall. That hurts, but he looks back down the other side of the room and he's left the door open. He waits for the other side of the room to rise and when it does he gets to the door and shuts it and holds onto it long enough to lock it. Then he feels his way into the bathroom. The bathroom has leveled out and he reaches down into the warm bath water for a bottle of beer. But the room pitches behind him again and he lands in the bathtub, head first. Head first, body following right behind, Chester lands in the water and lies there in the bobbing warm beer bottles.

He looks up at the ceiling with sharp pain in his forehead and he says something out loud.

"OK. *I think that will be enough.*"

He laughs.

"Yes," he says again out loud, "I think that will just about do it."

And he falls asleep in the bathtub, in the cold water and the bottles of beer.

He's smiling.

ENOUGH

AGAIN, TONIGHT, RAIN. This time hissing down on Dingle. Again, everyone in bed under the rooftops, under the blankets. One of them stares at the ceiling, listening to the dripping rain, glad for the shelter.

But now his memories are dripping too.

The old man gets out of bed slowly, trying not to rock the mattress and wake his wife, who's snoring. He eases himself up from the bed listening to her, moving with her snoring rhythm, hoping she doesn't stop. She doesn't, he smiles in the dark, slips on a robe, turns the doorknob, and only when he's down the hall does he breathe again.

At the end of the hall is a softly lit lamp framed in the doorway of the reading and TV lounge, and he aims for it, walking softly. The old man passes Chester's door, slows down and listens a moment, walks on.

In the lounge now, he relaxes. There's a snack bar and tea setup here, and he makes a cup of Earl Grey, breathing in the steam, sipping as it cools. The old man sits back in a big chair and crosses his bare feet on the coffee table, kicking aside some plastic toy cars. There's a long white scar along his right wrist and forearm running up under his robe sleeve and he remembers how it happened.

It happened in this bed and breakfast, early in his marriage, years and years ago, a night like this, his wife already in bed down the hall, same room, him awake and wandering out into the rain, into a pub, staying too long like always, coming back zig-zagging and starting up the stairs, everything tilting, him falling backwards down the stairs to the landing, getting angry and embarrassed about falling like that, getting to his feet, stumbling into the dark pub there at the foot of stairs, picking up a pint glass and smashing it and his hand down on the bar.

And after that, all the lights were on and everybody, including his wife, came running down the stairs, and they could all see his blood on the floor from the arm he's looking at tonight.

The old man knows what he was really mad about that night. It wasn't just about falling down the stairs. He was mad that night because he was doing what they all had always done, on and on and on, all the men in the family, and the women home and tolerating the on and on and on. Sometimes. Sometimes they didn't. Sometimes the women joined in with the on and on and on.

It wasn't even so much wrong and hurtful as finally just boring. Predictable. Not very good times, but normal.

But tonight it's rain on the roof, a hot cup of tea resting on his belly, a warm, fluffy robe, and that same woman down the hall. This old man is at peace, there's nowhere to go except back down the hall. What a relief.

He's awake and remembering all of this because of meeting Chester earlier tonight.

The old man is tired. He hopes Chester will get smart, like he did. He wants to say something to him. But now it's back to bed. He gets up from the chair, finishes the tea, and rinses the cup. He takes a fresh packet of Earl Grey, rips it open, walks down the hall to Chester's door, and drapes the bag on the doorknob by the string.

It's something anyway, he's thinking, a gesture or a hint; something he would've liked finding in the morning, a bit strange maybe, and he puts a hand on the door and says, "Good night, lad."

He creaks down the hall to his room, turns the doorknob slowly, slips off the robe, eases down onto the mattress slowly in time with her snoring, and is in bed with his wife again.

MAYBE YOU STAYED OUT too late in Dingle tonight and didn't get a room. You were at the pub and you had one and then another and then another and you kept talking and watching everybody and the music didn't stop and there were good-looking people looking back at you and then you saw a clock. You got out the door and the rain woke you up a bit but the streets back to the bed and breakfast were nothing but tilting mazes.

But you did get back there.

Too late to check in now, you know it, so you stand across the street and look at the building, all the lights out. It's really warm in there, people are sleeping like you need to right now. You might wake someone up in there to give you a room tonight but it wouldn't be right, getting someone out of bed this early in the morning.

So you'll keep walking around tonight. And it's really ok. And you don't worry. Those doors will be open in the morning.

It's early, but it's not too late.

WELCOME TO IRELAND!

CHESTER IS UP early. He takes off his clothes, squeezes as much water as he can out of them, drains the bathtub, loads the beer bottles into a bag, showers, and gets back into his damp, cold clothes. Everything is neat and clean in the room, and the sun shines in through the window. He's got a big headache, but he's whistling. On the way out of the room, he finds the teabag on the doorknob.

"Well, well," he says, grinning. "Dingle Room Service!"

He twirls the teabag on a finger and whistles his way down the hall to breakfast.

Chester's at a window table in the dining room with his teabag in hot water. He's looking out over the bay and watches as a little truck pulls up, two men get out, unload a big tangled net, and begin to lay it out on the pier. It looks like hard, *tangled*, agonizing work to Chester, but the men are laughing even as they get snagged and tripped up in the net. As he watches them, he smells perfume in the room. He turns and sees the old couple from last night sit down at a table in the corner. They smile and wave good morning, and drink tea. Chester waves at them but looks back out the window and watches the two men with the net, who seem to be having so much fun, working.

"I couldn't help noticing your accent last night, Chester." It's the old man talking to him. " You say you're from Cork?"

"Yes. Of course, I've only been there about a week."

"When are you going back to America?"

"I'm not."

This seems to take the old couple by surprise. It seems to take Chester by surprise as well, but he's smiling when he says it. The old couple look at each other and then back at Chester. They're smiling too. The old woman raises her teacup.

"Welcome to Ireland!" she says. Now the old man raises his cup.

"And you've chosen a good city in Cork. Good old Cork. Good old *Rebel Cork!*"

Chester says goodbye, goes to his room, gets the bag of beer, and leaves the bed and breakfast.

The sky is blue and a cold wind is blowing hard across Dingle. Chester walks out towards the harbor with his bag. He nods good morning to the two men now folding the huge net and they nod back. Being early, it's quiet out here too, just the bumping sound of hulls against the docks, water splashing, wind, seagulls, and bells. Chester walks on past the two men to their little pickup truck, which has one door hanging open. The men have moved very far from their truck with all their untangling and folding of the net.

Standing behind the truck, Chester pretends to take in the wide view of the Dingle harbor and all the boats and the seagulls and every beautiful Dingle thing in sight, but he's *really* watching the two men working. Chester quietly puts the paper bag into the truck bed. He starts walking back down the pier, slowly, casually, even taking out his wallet and pretending it's a camera, taking pictures with it, still being at a distance from the men.

As Chester gets nearer to the men one of them smiles and this time says hello.

"On holiday, are you?" he asks.

Chester says, "Yes, but today's the last day. Back to it tomorrow. See ya."

Chester has a fifteen-minute wait at the bus stop, and as he waits the two men fold the net over and over onto itself — down the pier. When they finish this, they lift the net together, slowly turn, and look down the pier to the pickup truck now far away.

"For fuck's sake. Better fold it the other direction next time!" says the older one, and they drop the net on the pier. The younger man walks to the truck, cursing but laughing. The older man sees Chester at the bus stop and waves, shrugging and laughing about the net and the truck so far away. Chester shrugs and laughs. And he hears a bus coming.

The bus stops with a hiss and Chester waves goodbye to the old fisherman. He pays the driver for his ticket and, moving down the bus aisle, watches the little pickup truck back up to the net and the older man. Chester sits on the harbor side of the bus and slides the window open. He watches as the truck stops close to the net, and the young man gets out. The bus driver closes the front door. The young man walks around to the back of the truck and lowers the tailgate. He stands there looking in the bed of the truck, then reaches in and picks up the bag. The bus driver starts his engine. The older man walks over and they each take out a bottle of beer. When they look up at the bus slowly pulling away, they see Chester in his bus window, smiling.

The bottles are raised high over their heads as the bus drives out of Dingle, over the hill, back towards Cork.

WHEN THE WETLANDS CALL

THE MORNING COMES in the window sunny and windy and with a lot of fresh, clean, cold air.

Sondra and Tommy have left the bedroom window open overnight, and green lacy curtains blow over them in bed. Tommy lies awake, watching them sail overhead, fluttering.

He's been wide awake and smiling at the ceiling for hours though every bit of his body is all the way and *delightfully* worn out.

Sondra's softly snoring and Tommy feels something big has just happened to him. Something that might be with him for the rest of his life. Sondra looks like forever to him. This is what he's feeling and he knows that his feelings have pushed him around his whole life. Some people didn't think that was such a good thing, they told Tommy he should think things through more. But look where I am this morning, he is thinking, because of these feelings.

Not bad, he is thinking. Or feeling. Or both.

Tommy smells sleeping Sondra's hair in a wild tangle under the wine-stained sheets. He looks down below her tangled hair to her round white ass with bits of strawberry jam smeared on each cheek. Tommy doesn't remember what day it is and neither does he remember why she has strawberry jam on her ass, but he smiles. He looks again at her hand, at the freckles and tiny scars on her fingers, the bright red fingernail polish mostly scraped away. He listens to her slow sleepy breathing, and snoring, takes her hand, sniffs it, and inhales a combination of peachy skin cream, her perfume, and the smell of sex.

Tommy hears his underpants ticking on top of Sondra's old wind-up grandfather clock. He looks around; everywhere are bottles and glasses and CDs and bits of clothing, over on the window sill there's a chunk of cheese with a knife stuck in and next to it a tube of lubricating jelly squeezed flat. Near his head is Sondra's bra, he drapes it across his face. It smells like cloves and, like the strawberry jam, he can't remember why *this* would be the case, but he's very glad about his situation this morning.

Tommy kisses Sondra's hand, takes a good long look at it, thinking he'll be holding this hand for the rest of his life, then closes his eyes and is back asleep in a minute.

And another minute after that, Sondra wakes up. She stretches and smiles in the sheets and smells the clean clear cold river air blowing in through the window. She looks up at the green curtains blowing over the bed. They are made from an old dress of hers. She remembers the night she ripped this dress off, in a very real sort of *direct invitation* to a musician guest for the night, a shy guy from Dublin, down in Cork for a weekend gig. In the morning, all their clothes on the floor and this dress in shreds, the dress looked to her like something to remember the night by.

The musician went back to Dublin and Sondra made new curtains.

She looks at this new musician in her bed, asleep and slightly smiling, Nepo asleep with him, rising and falling on Tommy's stomach. She's thinking maybe this guy will bring her more than curtains.

Sondra tip-toes naked over to the window and looks out at clear blue sky and trees whipping around. It's been wet and windy for days now, the sky and the weather changing every hour, it seems to her. She can see the dog yard from her bedroom window behind the shelter, and the dogs are unusually busy and running around each other and playing. One of them jumps up in the air after a yellow leaf that rides up and down on the wind.

This is going to be a good day, she thinks, as she puts on her red dress. One of Nepo's ears goes up as he watches from

Tommy's stomach. He's watching her but he'll wait; he knows to make his move when Sondra starts towards the door, jingling keys. This is going to be a good couple of days, she thinks, dabbing on some perfume. I'm not sure what's going to happen, she thinks, but *something's* coming.

She looks at the bottle of perfume and starts laughing. *Wet Foggy Bog* it's called. Strange name for a perfume, she still thinks. She remembers the first time she saw it in an advert in the Irish Times with a nearly naked man and an almost completely naked woman walking, of course—barefoot—in mist, hand in hand, in mud along a lakeside. And under the picture—*Wet Foggy Bog. For Women ... When The Wetlands Call.*

Sondra laughs again, can't believe anyone actually got away with that stupid ad, and dabs a bit more Wet Foggy Bog down between her breasts. Stupid ad, yet when she looks over at Tommy's big foot and hairy ankle sticking out of her sheets and remembers last night, she has to admit she *can* hear the wetlands calling.

She writes a note for Tommy, puts on her sunglasses, jingles her keys, and Nepo shoots off Tommy's stomach!

CHESTER COMES HOME

CHESTER WAKES UP as the bus rolls into the Cork bus depot. It has been the best sleep he's had in a very long time. He's been dreaming of seagulls in his sleep and now he looks up through the bus windows at the pigeons wheeling over the river and depot. It's sunny and bright and the buildings seem to be glowing in Chester's eyes.

He's the last one to get off and stands a moment in the door of the bus and watches everybody walking around on the street, blown along by the wind. He looks up over the depot and across the River Lee up the hill to the street of houses where he lives.

Chester steps down from the bus and walks in that direction, passing the animal shelter. He smiles, taking long, slow steps. He knows he has apologies to make to Kieran and Rob and Tommy but that's fine with him. He *will* apologize. He's even looking forward to them being pissed off at him for leaving Cork without a word. And walking along, thinking happily about them all yelling at him pretty soon, he comes to a very large poster, with a photograph of Tommy in the center, stapled to a wooden pole.

The pole is just past the front door of the animal shelter, and in the slightly fuzzy photograph Tommy stands on a hillside. It's shot from a low angle and he's looking off into the distance, seemingly with a lot on his mind, his soul at its absolute depth, his musical cup runneth over, holding a microphone with a cord trailing off in the grass to somewhere.

Also off in the grass, on the very edge of the photograph, Chester can just make out Rob, not quite cropped out of the image, looking like he's laughing and encouraging Tommy.

Chester shakes his head and starts laughing. An old woman elbows past him on the sidewalk but he stops her and says, "I *know* this guy!" She keeps moving but then she stops and looks back over her shoulder, frowning and shaking her fist at Chester.

"Do *I* not know someone? I dated a Chieftain before he was put up on a pole like your friend there, so ..."

Chester's about to say—*That's wonderful! We have a little something in common*—but before he can, she daintily pulls her skirt up the back of her legs a few inches and makes a farting sound with her mouth. And then she's gone, walking bow-legged down the sidewalk.

Chester looks back at the pole. On the poster, over the photograph of Tommy, are big black letters.

!TOMMY LIVE!
SONGBIRD OF CORK
Saturday night, 8 until ?
Shane's Pub

Saturday. Tomorrow night. It will be a big night for Tommy. Chester crosses the street and starts walking dreamily down the street, smiling broadly, right out in public, about how brave Tommy is to do this, and how free he'll feel when it's all over. *The moment he begins to sing!* Chester's wandering around with all this in his head, turns down an alley, comes out on the next street, and when he looks up, here comes the bow-legged old woman again, still shaking her fist at him, still mouth-farting at him!

Chester snaps out of his reverie, blows her what he hopes she receives as a heartfelt kiss, runs back up the alley and back to the poster of Tommy on the pole. He reads it again, this time all the way down to the bottom.

A Rob & Declan Tommy Show, Inc., Ltd.
Cork, Ireland

OUR MOTTO
Just when you thought you were
sleeping
and dreaming
but that your alarm hasn't gone off yet
and that your dreams aren't going to
come true and
then you wake up and there they are,
COMING TRUE!

Chester smiles at the lines. Leave it to Rob to come up with a catchy, succinct motto, he thinks. Then he walks across the bridge, up the hill to his stone house. He's home.

SONDRA PLUS JULIE EQUALS CHAMPAGNE

NEXT DOOR to Shane's Pub is a cozy, wooden, brown and yellow tea shop; Julie's in the window seat sipping tea and watching the river, something she's learned to do in the last year or so. Her friends are doing yoga, but she likes to stare at the river for at least twenty minutes a day and she gets the same thing they do. She's had her twenty minutes, so now she's sketching on a pad with a fountain pen. She's laying out Tommy's stage and how the decorations will hang and where the chairs will be in front of the stage.

She looks at the river again. It amazes her how well this river-staring thing works. Julie pours tea and goes back to her sketch pad, drawing a figure of Tommy at the microphone. She leans back and squints at the drawing and she likes it. She has the whole room laid out and the band on the stage and even some figures standing and cheering from the floor.

"Is that Tommy?" Julie jumps in her chair at the question and turns around to a woman standing behind her wearing sunglasses and grinning down at the sketchpad. Julie realizes she's been smelling a musky perfume these last few minutes and now she knows it's coming from this woman in the sunglasses. Sondra looks at the empty chair at Julie's table, asks, "May I?" and sits down. The waitress brings a cup of tea and Sondra takes off her sunglasses.

"Are you part of the Tommy Show? I mean, I'm going next door to Shane's in a minute to help set up, and when I saw your drawing there I thought you must be with the show! My name is Sondra." Julie stares at Sondra now instead of the river. This woman, who is going next door in a minute to help set up, sits across the table in a red dress that opens up low on her breasts, and she's wearing purple suede boots. Julie starts to laugh and thinks that this looks like a new friend.

"Yes Sondra, I'm sort of a friend of Tommy's. I'm Julie. And yes, that is him. Do you know him as well?"

Sondra gives Julie a long, slow look that tells her just how well she knows Tommy. Julie reaches across the table and the two shake hands.

"Brilliant, Sondra. Tommy's a good man, isn't he? And a grand singer."

Julie and Sondra study each other a moment, then Julie says, "Funny we've not met before in Cork. Have you always lived here?"

Sondra leans back in her chair and lays one purple-booted foot on the table. "Pretty much mostly always have. Not born here, but here I am," says Sondra. "And you?" Sondra looks out the window and waits for Julie's answer.

"Yeah, me too." Julie looks out the window too. At Cork, and at the river. There's a little dog in the window now, looking back and forth between her and Sondra. "Is that your dog?"

"Nepo. My best friend in Cork. Well until, you know, the new one. The two-legged, musical one. Sometimes three-legged." Sondra squints at Julie now, smiling, and jiggling her purple boot on the table. "And I have a feeling I may be looking at another. Have you had anything to eat? What about us two having a real breakfast? Enough of these tea biscuits."

So they order an even *fuller* Full Irish than usual. And after awhile they are laughing so much that the other customers start laughing, and then the waitress is laughing, and the cook comes out of the kitchen and it had been such a quiet morning until these two met.

Nepo is invited inside, takes a blood sausage from Sondra and runs under the table. The cook brings a plate of scraps from the kitchen, slides it under the table, and that's the last they see of Nepo. The cook and the waitress look at each and smile, open a bottle of champagne, sit down with Sondra and Julie, the other customers come over and sit down, and the **CLOSED** sign goes up on the door.

PUT YOUR GODDAMN SHOES ON

UP IN THE STONE HOUSE, Chester wakes up from a long nap, and he is absolutely happy for no reason for the first time in a long time. He can't believe he feels this good and so he starts to think about this and how can he hold onto it? And as he starts to stare at the ceiling and lies in bed just a little too long, he gradually begins to feel bad for no reason, and his eyes glaze over.

Oh yeah, this. This, he remembers. This thing in my head again, he remembers, he remembers *this* all right. Then he remembers something else.

Don't think alone. His eyes blink and he's up and out of bed getting dressed.

Why not just feel happy for no reason? And with no thinking about it one way or the other? Not that easy, says one voice in his head. Put your goddamn shoes on, says another. This may be a profound new philosophy of life you're having, says a third voice, but you're going to need some outside help with it.

Yet another voice wonders if, with all these voices talking to him, maybe he's losing his mind?

"Probably," says Chester, out loud, as he slams the front door and *flies* down the street towards Cork.

Chester stops first at Rob's house, knocks, nobody home. Then he walks over to Tommy's, knocks. Same again. He crosses the River Lee, walks up the hill along Sunday's Well Road, in the direction of Kieran's Inn. He doesn't walk very far before he hears the sound of a motor right behind him, idling, then switching off, and then the big shotgun backfire.

Chester looks ahead, down the road, out over the hills surrounding Cork. Slowly, he raises his arms overhead in surrender, turns around, and there's Kieran with his chin on the steering wheel, looking at him. Chester smiles, drops his arms, walks back and gets in the van. Kieran still has his chin on the wheel, looking straight ahead. A long moment passes.

"And what was that about, then?" Kieran still looking down the road. Chester looks down there too.

"I went out to Dingle for a day." Kieran leans back in his seat now and takes a deep breath, but keeps his eyes down the road.

"Go out there to figure things out, did you? All that stuff you've been talking about?" Chester can sense Kieran looking at him out of the corner of his eye so he nods yes but he keeps looking straight ahead. Finally, they turn and look at each other.

Kieran looks angry and worried but there's something else there that's on the edge of laughter about all this seriousness and punishing silence. Kieran looks down the road again.

"So. Did you figure it all out?"

"No, Kieran, nothing was figured out whatsoever."

"Nothing? No secrets discovered, no wisdom won?"

"Don't think alone."

"Don't think alone. Don't you mean ..."

"Nope. That's what he said."

"Who?"

"A barman."

"Don't think alone. Anything else?"

"That's about it."

Kieran turns and really looks at Chester now.

"Not bad. I'll have to think about that one."

He reaches across Chester and takes a pair of glasses from the glove box and puts them on. Chester has never seen him in these glasses or any glasses, and these glasses are very *ugly*. Huge plastic brown frames and so many scratches across the lenses it's like looking at Kieran's eyes through a screen door.

Chester smiles at Kieran's joke to ease the conversation. The glasses come off and Kieran puts his hand out to shake.

"Good to see you again, Chester. I'm glad you're back."

They shake hands, Kieran flings the joke glasses over his shoulder into the back seat and they look ahead through the windshield again in silence for a moment.

"Well, now that we have that all sorted out, let's take these loaner amplifiers to Shane's for the show." And Kieran starts the motor and makes a u-turn back towards town.

Chester is about to break into a laughing fit. For whatever reason, everything feels funny now. But he's trying to hold the laughter back. A soccer ball bounces into the street and Kieran swerves so wide of it he almost drives into the river, and now Chester cannot hold back the laughter. Kieran hears this and smiles a little himself but he's pondering something.

"Dingle, eh? I was there a long time ago and some fella told me something, it was kind of a piece of advice. What was it? It was a kind of a pun or something, a witticism. Oh yeah. It was this. He said, 'Never dangle too long in Dingle.'"

Chester shakes with laughter, trying to breathe. Kieran keeps driving and tries to look serious, like he's just quoted Yeats, but now he's starting to laugh.

"God only knows what *that* was supposed to mean," he says.

CROOKED AND SIDEWAYS

KIERAN AND CHESTER drive over to Shane's Pub, the Kieran's Inn Shuttle Van nearly dragging on the street under the weight of the big black amplifiers in the back.

Chester is still laughing. Kieran sings a song that he's making up as he drives, hitting the steering wheel with the chorus—*Don't Dangle in Dingle, Don't Dangle in Dingle*, and as he pulls the van over to the curb behind Declan's car, he runs into the back bumper with a crash and a backfire.

Declan and Rob run out of the pub and look across the street. Kieran waves at them. Chester gets out of the van.

Chester meets Rob between the smashed bumpers and puts a hand out for Rob to shake.

"Hello, Rob. Hello friend. I am sorry. I'm sorry I didn't say anything and left Cork like I did. I was sort of crooked and sideways and inside my brain. So, I went to Dingle. I've been crooked and sideways a long time and I went to Dingle on the bus. My brain, it's been crooked and sideways and I've been inside there for years but I think it's time to straighten it out, sort of air it out, you know what I mean? Am I making any sense whatsoever?"

Rob nods yes.

"Well, anyway, even if I don't make any sense, it is very good to see you again, Rob." Chester starts towards the back of the van but Rob stops him. He takes Chester by his shoulder, and squeezes it.

"Very, very good to see you as well, Chester. I'm glad you're back. And I do understand what you've just said. It's hard to say that stuff. But just between you and me, I'm *still* crooked and sideways. I found the right place—here, in Cork —to be that way, out in the open!"

The license plate falls off Declan's dented bumper, Rob and Chester give each other a hug, and Kieran gets out of the van, singing.

"... Dangling too long in Dingle will get you in a tangle, but Dingling a bit in Dangle will surely bring a tingle ..."

Then he opens the back of the van, nods to Chester, and together they carry a very large amplifier into Shane's Pub.

Kieran still singing, still working on the song.

A LONG BLACK LIMOUSINE

KIERAN AND CHESTER and Rob and Declan are in a cheerful circle trying to untangle long electrical cords from the back of Kieran's van when a long black limousine drives slowly by, slowly, almost stopping, then drives on past. Kieran and Chester and Rob go on untangling.

Declan watches the car.

He tells the others he's going for a walk.

He walks to the part of Cork where his office is. When he gets to this street, the black limousine is parked in front of the building.

It's also parked alongside three Smart cars, blocking them in, and a large man in a suit is leaning against the limo, looking up at the building and yelling into a cell phone. He has white hair and it's combed back, neat and slick and shiny.

Declan is at the corner of the block and ducks back out of sight. The sky has gone grey and misty and he stares down the street, which is also grey. The pub across the street from him has grey stone walls and Declan thinks about all the grey he's looking at. He chuckles and says to himself, "Alright, don't *you* go grey, too."

He peeks around the corner. The man is off the phone and pacing on the sidewalk. Declan pulls back out of sight again and leans his head against the wall. The wall is wet and bright green moss is growing on the bricks. He touches the moss delicately with shaking fingers and then he walks around the corner.

The man sees Declan coming and stops pacing, smiles pleasantly, but doesn't move towards him. Declan smiles as big as he can and walks right to the man in the suit, who looks back up at the building. They both speak at the same time.

Declan says, "Good morning, father, good to see you!"

His father says, "How's business?"

Only Declan has noticed that they have talked over each other and he puts a hand out for his father to shake, who repeats his question.

"How's business?"

And they stand there, Declan looking at him and the man still looking at the building. There's a driver sitting in the limo, looking straight ahead.

Declan feels like he's been in this spot before but he waits and doesn't care that his hand is shaking now.

And finally his father, after a little more dramatic silence, looks at Declan and speaks.

"I've not heard from you."

"No. You haven't. Nor I from you."

"Can you possibly tell me why, Declan? I don't think you know how I feel. How badly I feel about you. I worry about you and I try so hard to help, and yet my efforts to help you are consistently a waste of my time. You're my son, but I don't know what to do. I've tried so hard to understand you. And I don't."

Declan's father points at the building with his cell phone.

"I suppose everything is up there. Have you even unpacked? And I continue to pay for all of it? Am I right?"

Declan looks at the driver, who stares straight ahead behind the wheel.

"Father, I'm sorry for the expense and it is all still up there, yes. There's been a change. Of heart. And I will help you to get it moved, I will make the phone calls and—"

Declan stops because his father has moved suddenly and is standing right in front of him with a finger in his face.

"*Oh* no! YOU are going to make phone calls and get it all arranged and taken care of? Is that it? YOU will do all of this? Is that what you are saying to me now? That you will take care of it? A change of heart? This office I set up for you and all the other things I've tried to help you with for years? And you've had a change of heart?"

He shakes his head sweetly and sympathetically, pats Declan on the head, and dials a number on his cell phone.

"I don't think so, son." He turns away from Declan as his phone rings someone somewhere else.

"Could you repeat that please?" Declan asks.

The father turns around and looks at Declan, the phone still ringing.

"That last word. What was it again?"

His father stops the call and shrugs. "I couldn't say."

"Son. The word was son."

"Yes. Right. That was the word I used. Now what?"

"I just wanted to hear it one more time."

Declan's father laughs a little, but he's interrupted from behind by a young man and his girlfriend who ask very kindly how long he will be because their car is blocked by the limousine.

"It'll be when I get done here if that's at all acceptable to you." The young couple look at Declan and then walk back over to their car and wait for whatever is happening in front of them to be over. Declan's father glares at them and then he turns the glare back on Declan.

"Explain for me, if you will, what has possessed you to let this *yet another* opportunity go? I saw you there on the street with some people doing I don't know *what* in front of a pub and then of course you deign to skulk over here and talk to me. What are you thinking? I don't know what is in your mind."

Declan looks at the limousine driver.

"You never have and you never will," he says, walking over to the driver's window. He looks in at the driver who keeps looking down the street.

"Hello, Donal. Come on. Say something. It is very good to see you, you know. You look good, even in that stupid chauffeur suit." The chauffeur drops his shoulders and lets out a huge blast of breath, laughs, and shakes hands with Declan.

"And you, Declan, fuckin' Christ I've missed you, you fuck," and Donal takes off his sunglasses. "Very, very good to see you too. What'll we do now?"

Declan looks across the top of the limo at his father who's back on the phone yelling and walking up and down the sidewalk, then he looks at the young couple waiting in their car. Declan leans back down into Donal's window.

"You like music don't you, Donal?"

"Fuckin' hell, who doesn't?"

"Would you like a job with a band?"

"Doin' what?"

Declan doesn't know the answer.

"You can start by backing this car up and letting those kids out, right?"

Donal does this and the kids drive away waving while Declan's father, still yelling into the phone and very red in the face, spins around and yells now at his chauffeur.

"What in HELL are you doing?"

Donal parks the limo and gets out. Declan points at Donal's tightly knotted black tie and Donal takes it off.

The father, walking towards the limo stops suddenly, hearing something on the phone that makes him even angrier.

"What? WHAT DID YOU JUST SAY TO ME?" And then he's pacing again.

"Let's go," says Declan.

Donal looks at his boss on the sidewalk, absorbed on the cell phone with someone, somewhere else. "Right," he says, and drops the black tie on the street.

After they walk in silence for awhile, Donal asks, "You're working for a band?"

"Yes. A sort of co-manager for a singer, really. A great voice."

"And you can get me a job with him as well, can you?"

"Yeah, of course."

A bit more walking, then Donal has another question.

"Where am I going to live?" Donal stops and looks back. Declan takes him by the arm and pulls him ahead.

"Come on, Donal. With me. With me, for as long as you need to. Come on."

Silence as they walk along.

"I can't believe I allowed my own father to make me the manager of a Holiday Inn."

Declan and Donal stop and look at each other.

"At least you didn't chauffeur your own father all over Ireland," says Donal.

"True." says Declan.

"Can we get a drink somewhere?"

"Oh yes. We can. Let's go."

And they start walking again.

TOMMY ON THE FERRY AGAIN, DREAMING

SATURDAY MORNING, minutes after midnight.

The wild sea wind blows rain into Tommy's face and he's on that ferry again, heaving across the dark wee-hour waves of the Irish Sea. He hears the music and he can see the little red and blue lights far away on the surface of the water, but this time he's on solid ground and he's not alone. He has Nepo with him, and they're in Cork, standing on the corner, looking across the street to Shane's Pub.

"Won't be long now, little friend," he says down to Nepo, shivering wet and low with muddy paws on the sidewalk, also looking across the street to the pub.

And over there, across the street in Shane's Pub, Sondra and Julie, and Chester and Rob and Kieran and Declan and Donal are sitting at a long table, listening to the rain, talking about Tommy's show. Sondra looks up at the dark stage.

"Think we're ready?" she asks. Rob smiles at her, and clinks her wine glass with his pint glass.

"Ready," he says. "So is Tommy, you know." Rob leans his chair back against the wall, takes a drink, and looks across the table. "Isn't he, Chester?"

Chester and Kieran and Declan and Julie all say *yes* at once, yes he is, that's right, lifting their glasses and toasting. Donal hasn't met Tommy yet, but he lifts his glass and says *yes*, too.

"So am I," says Rob, smiling.

"Me too," says Chester.

"As am I," says Declan, suddenly. "I saw him singing in the street. I needed to hear that. That day, I needed to hear that. I needed something like this to happen, you know?"

Kieran and Julie smile at him, *yes, we know.*

Sondra, tonight without her sunglasses on, has tears in her eyes.

"Well, hell, I'm ready as well," she says. "I'm ready for another round if it's not too late!"

"Not TONIGHT it's not!" yells Rob and his chair hits the floor.

He and Chester go to the bar.

Outside, Tommy picks up Nepo and slides him inside his coat, leaving the little head out between the lapels, looking around, blinking and shaking off the rain. Tommy feels the little dog shaking hard inside his coat but Nepo looks up and licks Tommy on the chin. Tommy walks across the street and taps on the window. His friends look up and raise their glasses to him and Nepo. Nepo raises his ears and paws at the window. Sondra winks at Tommy.

Tommy goes to his apartment and gets a box out of the closet. He leaves the apartment and, back out in the rain, carries the box inside his coat with Nepo. In a few minutes, he's through the door of the shelter.

"Let's go to bed," Tommy says, and carries the dog to bed and to dreams.

Dreams both tonight and tomorrow.

IF YOU HAPPEN TO BE in the Cork bus station tonight, you're about to see something funny.

The station is empty when a bus swings in and stops. The front door opens and the driver gets off, shaking his head, and walks into the station. He takes off his bus driver's hat and throws it on the ticket counter, waves his hand at the clerk like he is giving up being a driver, and walks through a door that says "Employees Only."

Outside, you can see a bunch of men inside the bus walking up the aisle to the door. The first man climbs out in a black suit carrying a guitar case and falls down the steps of the bus. The other men, five in all, all in black suits too, are so close behind him that they fall over him as he falls down, and they all land in a pile. The guitar case of the first man hits the parking lot and opens and the guitar skids all the way into the wall of the bus station and breaks a string.

All the men lying in the pile look at that and are silent. Then the first man that fell looks at his guitar and speaks.

"What do you think it means? Is it some kind of omen or sign?"

The men are beginning to stand up and brush themselves off because, tired as they look, the bus station parking lot is no bed.

One of the others answers the question.

"Yes. It is a sign. It does mean something."

"What?"

"If God be for us, who can be Guinness?"

The men get up and brush themselves off, walk into the station and sit down.

"What is that supposed to mean?" one of them asks, then goes to sleep.

THE LITTLE RED ROOSTERS

THE SUN COMES UP on Cork and it's a beautiful morning. The rain has blown off to the south and the old city is cleaned off and gleaming new. The sky is blue and wide and seems to go all the way up there forever, which, of course, it does.

It's Saturday morning and people are walking a little quicker, a little more nimbly, and as they walk along in all directions towards all their things to do, they breathe in the cold clean air and their eyes are gleaming new too.

Last night is gone, good morning to you!

At the bus station though, unaware of this rejuvenating dawn, five men in matching black suits have passed out and are sleeping, leaning against each other on a bench. It's been a long night on the bus from Castlebar but they've made it and they have their instruments with them.

Also at the bus station, absolutely aware of this rejuvenating dawn, five men in non-matching clothes walk up to the bench and wait for someone sleeping there to wake up.

Kieran studies the men in black and after awhile he says, "They look like black crows sleepin' on a telephone line, don't they Chester?"

Chester agrees with this and says, "Is this them, Rob?"

Rob nods but checks with Declan, "I recognize them. Don't you?"

Declan nods and looks at his brother, trying to include him as the new partner, but Donal says, "I just got here, you know."

The men on the bench begin to wake up and stretch and as they look up and begin to focus on the men standing in front of them it gets very quiet. And it continues to be very quiet.

Tommy walks into the station in a white bathrobe. His face is rosy red and his hair is combed back from a shower he's had at Sondra's, in her apartment in the animal shelter across the street.

"Everybody ready?" he sings into the quiet.

Everybody looks at each other.

Tommy turns to Rob standing with Chester and Kieran and Declan and Donal. "Ready, Rob?" he asks. Rob puts on his sunglasses and looks serious.

"I'm ready, Tommy."

And now the five black crows struggle off the bench and the most awake of them moves forward.

"We're ready too, Tommy."

And everybody shakes hands, introducing themselves all around. Tommy watches as the ten men shake hands with each other. And they go on shaking hands to make sure they've met everybody and they keep on with it so long that complete strangers in the station come and join in, to be a part of all this friendliness. But, at last, it's just the ten again and Tommy says, "Come on then. Let's go."

Kieran and Chester lead the musicians out to the Kieran's Inn Shuttle Van where Julie and Sondra sit in the front seat talking and laughing. They stop talking as this incongruous gang of men approaches the van, but they don't stop laughing.

In fact, looking at these men, they *can't* stop.

Tommy in his bathrobe, Rob, Chester, Kieran, Declan, the five sleepy musicians in black suits bumping into each other and squinting in the morning sunlight, and then there's this new guy Donal, still wearing his limo driver uniform and cap.

Julie, still laughing, asks the musicians what they are called.

"We are—The Little Red Roosters," says the least sleepy one, and Kieran winks at Julie.

"That's a good name for a band," she says. "My Dah would've liked you guys."

The musicians are barely standing.

Tommy nods at the large pile of instrument cases. "Looks to me like you lads could use some rest. We'll take care of your stuff. We'll carry it over to Shane's."

The Little Red Roosters nod and climb into the van and Julie drives them out to Kieran's Inn to five free rooms, where the musicians fall asleep in their clothes until the afternoon rehearsals.

Chester picks up the guitar, Rob the sax, Kieran carries the big upright bass, Declan and Donal bring the drums and handmade sheet music, and they all start walking towards Shane's Pub. Tommy says he'll meet them there in a few minutes, and goes across the street to the animal shelter to get dressed.

Alone now in Sondra's bedroom, Tommy looks under the bed and takes out the box he's brought from home. Inside is his special suit for tonight. The suit no one has seen yet, not Rob, not even Sondra. He takes the lid off the box and parts the tissue paper. He hasn't even worn the suit since the day he bought it months ago on Patrick Street. He remembers Jack, the man in the shop who sold him the suit and tailored it. "Jack O'Shea - Proprietor & Tailor" says the clean white business card still resting on the lapel inside the box. A skinny, sharp-dressed man with bright white hair combed back neat and shiny on his head with yellow teeth and lots of wrinkles crinkling back from his eyes every time he smiled, which, Tommy remembers, was *all the time*. Tommy loved that day.

"Jack, I need the most absolutely grandiose suit you have in the store!" he'd said. Jack was about half as tall as Tommy but still, he'd been able to put a fatherly hand up on his shoulder.

"What's the occasion then, son?"

"I'm going to be ... I AM a singer."

Jack had caught the change and he winked broadly at Tommy, clicking his tongue.

"That's the stuff, son! Come back here, I have just the one for you."

And this is the suit that Jack showed him. Tommy touches the fabric but puts the lid back on the box and the box back under the bed. He won't put it on yet. Tonight.

Then he sees an envelope on the floor, under the window, his name written on it. He gently opens the note.

Dear Tommy,

I love your voice and I cannot wait to see you EXPLODE on stage Saturday night! I believe in you, I'm proud of you, and ... by the way ...

I love you.

I have been waiting for you.
(What took you so damn long?!)

Je t'aime, your Sondra

p.s. Mister Songbird – you sure made ME sing last night!

Tommy sits down on the bed, holding the note. He reads it again, and looks out the window. The curtains are blowing again, and the cool, clean wind is in his face. He looks over at Sondra's dresser, her perfume bottles and jewelry tray. Her shoes kicked off on the floor, dresses and jeans, also on the floor. There's a photograph of her on the dresser; a little girl on a beach, sunglasses on, waving at the camera, hair blowing in the wind, smiling big. He reads the note again.

He sits there a long time.

LATER, the blue sky over Cork is about to give way to a
black line you see on the horizon and the wind is picking up.

CRACKLING, POPPING, SPARKLING;
TOMMY ONSTAGE!

THERE'S A HUM in the air. A crackling popping vibrating kind of burning electrical sound in the air.

All five of the Little Red Roosters are in their places on the stage at Shane's Pub. They look rested and alert, and their black suits are unbelievably sharp and immaculate considering they've been *traveled in* all night on the bus down the west coast of Ireland, then *slept in*, this morning.

Rob and Declan and Donal sit in the front row. After a few moments, Donal observes, "There seem to be many more amplifiers than musicians."

Kieran and Julie and Sondra walk into the pub and join the others in the front row. "What's that humming sound?" asks Julie. Kieran goes to the bar for six drinks.

Chester arrives and after his eyes adjust he goes over to Kieran at the bar.

"Drink, Chester?"

Chester smiles at Kieran. Then he laughs.

"No, Kieran, I believe I've had enough. Besides, *bathtubs* are for bathing."

Kieran looks at Chester, who's now trying to keep a straight face.

"Bathtubs are for bathing. Interesting idea, Chester. Very mysterious. Is it existential? Or does this have some connection to not dangling in Dingle?"

"A *direct* connection my friend," says Chester, and they carry the drinks back to the others and sit down.

Rob takes a long sip of stout and looks at the empty room behind them all.

"All those posters and flyers and everything and this is *it?*" Rob asks, rocking back and forth in his seat. The others want to comfort him, but it's true—behind them there's nobody but the bartender and two waitresses standing against the back wall. Kieran looks at Chester and they both step up on stage.

Kieran leans down close to the nearest musician and whispers, "Could you maybe, ehm—warm up?" This one, the *guitar* Rooster, looks out at the empty room, then turns to the band. He nods and they begin. The *drumming* and the *bass-playing* Roosters start working on a rhythm pattern and the *piano* Rooster tinkles in. The guitarist drops in with a slow riff and Kieran and Chester sit back down. The *sax-playing* Rooster doesn't hear anything to do yet so he sits and waits behind dark glasses. The bartender turns on the TV set and the two waitresses walk over from the back wall and watch the weather report.

The warm-up has cooled off.

Then Tommy walks in wearing his suit.

The front row is stunned, and the sax player takes off his shades.

As Tommy gets on stage and under the lights, he begins to sparkle. The suit is tinsel silver with red pinstripes and there's a glimmering from Tommy on the ceiling above the stage. Sondra's mouth is wide open.

Tommy looks long at Sondra from the stage. He takes her note from inside his silver jacket, holds it up for a moment, kisses it, slides it back inside and pats his jacket. He blows Sondra a kiss.

Sondra takes off her sunglasses, gives Tommy a big wink, then folds up the sunglasses and puts them on the table.

Tommy grabs the microphone stand and carries it to the front of the stage where he drops it and spreads out his glittering arms.

"Good evening, everybody! Thanks for comin'! My name is Tommy and straight from Castlebar, these are The Little!

Red! Roosters!" The bartender and two waitresses look up at the stage then turn back to the TV screen. "We're going to start the night with one you all know well ... 'The Irish Rover!' " Tommy turns to the band and counts, "One, two—one two three AND!"

The band starts the song with such sudden force that it startles everybody and Nepo runs under Sondra's chair.

The Roosters are on the attack. Smiling, but on the attack.

Tommy smiles too and his eyes are wildly looking out into the room, which is empty. He takes a very deep breath, his shoulders rise, and the voice that roars out of his mouth doesn't seem to care that the room is mostly empty. The voice, on the first verse, blasts through the room, through the window, and out into Cork.

The bartender runs around the bar to close the front door, and when he gets there a gang of young men is pushing past him, looking up at the stage. They order drinks and stand staring up at Tommy. They've heard this song all their lives; from their fathers and grandfathers and grandmothers singing it to hearing it on the radio, and in every pub they've ever been in. But they've never heard it like this and with this much volume, this much abandon.

The Little Red Roosters, half asleep this morning, are absolutely in synch and having the time of their lives. Or, at least, being a veteran band, another time of their lives. Everything shakes around them on stage; glasses of stout here and there on top of amplifiers are jiggling up heads of cream and spilling over, a little oscillating fan falls over and cools the back wall, and the drummer has already broken a drumstick.

The first song isn't even finished yet.

And Tommy keeps singing to that window daring Cork to come in.

Some of Cork is in that window, looking in and trying to get cover from the rain that's starting. The bartender looks up at the TV radar weather report, at a big storm moving over Cork, and he switches the set off. One of the guys that just arrived takes out a cell phone and walks back out the front door, past a man and a woman who come in clapping with the song. The couple is surprised there's no one in the pub except for some young men at the bar and a line of people in the very first row, clapping and stomping as the song comes to a crashing end. They applaud and look around for somewhere to sit. It's gotten suddenly quiet in the pub. They look up to the stage and Tommy smiles back at them, seemingly waiting for them. The Roosters are looking at them as well, and the drummer puts a hand behind his ear. The woman shrugs, giggling a little at all the attention, because not only the band but also that entire front row are all looking at her and smiling, and waiting.

Rob gets up and waves at her, coaxing her, and says, "What'll it be, darlin'?"

"Well uh, 'Whiskey In The Jar' maybe?" she says.

Tommy turns around, counts it off, and the band cranks up the song.

MUSIC, FROM SOMEWHERE

IN HER OFFICE at the Rose Lodge, Mary decides to call it a night. She's been doing paperwork on the computer. She hits the *save* button, but before she turns the computer off the lights in the room flicker off and on, then off altogether, and she hears the computer whir down to dead. There's silence now, except for rain on the window and some footsteps upstairs. This is cozy. She remembers the boxes of candles in the storeroom and hopes the power stays off. First, she'll pass out candles to the few guests in the lodge, then it'll be upstairs with a book in bed by candlelight and listen to the rain all night. A drink or two under the covers.

She hears the horse gallop of Eric running down the stairs and into her office.

"I have to say, Mary, I *love* this sort of night!" he says in the darkness. Now she hears Eric go out in the hall, open the fuse box, and flick the switches—nothing happens. She hears him come back.

"Me too, Eric!"

"I'll get the candles."

She hears him walking down the hall to the storeroom.

Mary pulls out a desk drawer and feels around for the flashlight and her silver whiskey flask. The flask is a gift from Phillip. The afternoon of the day he hired her, he asked her if she'd like to go out for tea, to celebrate.

"How about whiskey?" she'd said.

Phillip had been surprised, and for the second time that day. The first time was when she quoted the Beatles' lyric.

So, instead of tea, they went out for whiskey. And now, instead of the tea set Phillip was *going* to buy her, she has this flask, which she opens and sips from.

"Ah, *warm!*" she whispers, closing her eyes and leaning back in the chair.

Mary hears a saxophone somewhere, then the sound of more footsteps coming down the stairs. She flicks on the flashlight, goes into the hall, and aims the flashlight beam up into the stairway as her guests feel their way down.

Eric comes back with the candles and lights one for Mary's desk. The rain falls harder against the window, Mary passes the whiskey flask around to the guests, who squeeze into her little office. Even the non-drinkers drink, for warmth. And they all hear music coming from somewhere.

The wind creaks the old lodge and the guests get closer together in Mary's office. With Mary's whiskey, they're getting warmer. Eric puts on his hat.

"I'm going for Ellen. I'll be right back. Save some candlelight for us."

Mary goes to the window. Across the river, lights are on and shining along the hillside of houses. It's only the streets around the Rose Lodge that are in darkness. She watches Eric disappear into that dark.

THE LIGHTS GO OUT

THE PUB IS PACKED all the way to the back and out the door to the sidewalk. Tommy is out of his glittering coat. Chester is wearing it and dancing with Julie while Sondra dances with Rob. Kieran jumps up on stage with a fiddle nobody knew he owned let alone could play, another surprise tonight. Julie stops dancing and walks to the edge of the stage and gazes up at Kieran and she's laughing and crying both. Then she's back to dancing. Declan and Donal start off dancing with each other then switch to a couple of red-headed sisters who have been circling them in identical v-neck sweaters. The bartender has had to call for extra waitresses and he keeps a close watch on the red lights blinking on the sound equipment behind the band. He's not a musician so he doesn't know what these lights mean, but the music is so loud and the room is so wild with people, he worries that the place will blow a fuse.

He's wrong about that, but not really.

Tommy and the Roosters have played everything from Dubliners music to Chieftains to Van Morrison to Shane MacGowan to John Spillane to Sean Keane to Beatles and Stones and Louis Armstrong and Billie Holiday and Sinead O'Connor with people in the crowd coming up to sing with Tommy and nobody is at all tired.

Nobody but Nepo, somehow asleep under the drums.

Outside it is darker than usual. The rain is falling hard and a high wind from the sea is blowing water and everything and everybody sideways.

Eric too, blowing along sideways with Ellen, both of them laughing and wet, they stop to kiss and let themselves be knocked down to the ground by the wind, and so they do the kissing there, on a dark lawn. And they hear music through the wind. They lean up on elbows and see a faint yellow square of a window at Shane's Pub, people moving around within it. They kiss again, get up and walk splashing and laughing towards the window.

Pressing inside the pub, Ellen pulls Eric towards the bar and orders drinks. Up on stage, Tommy's suit tailor, Jack, is reading Yeats, his white hair glowing under the stage lights. The pub is silent as he takes his time reading "The Wild Old Wicked Man," which he reads from his trembling piece of paper at the microphone. When he is done, he walks to Tommy who hugs him and brings him back downstage to the microphone again. Tommy has his glimmering jacket on again. He points to it and then to the old man and back to the jacket again.

"This is Jack, everybody, the man who dressed me tonight. He clearly—CLEARLY—has poetic taste not only in verse but in *sainted sartorial splendor*. Looking at me, would you all be in agreement?"

The pub is very much in agreement. They are cheering.

Tommy holds up a hand. "AND! His shop is near to here. Patrick Street. Ask for Jack if you would like to look as grand as myself!"

The cheering goes on as Tommy and Jack huddle and talk on stage. Then they walk over to the piano player and the sax player joins the conversation. Kieran leans in listening along with the guitar player. They all nod and break off from the huddle and Tommy goes to the microphone again.

"Jack has a request." Jack also has a mandolin. Tommy looks back to the drummer who nods yes, ready. Tommy looks out over the room and calls out, "Give The Fiddler A Dram."

Tommy starts singing and the Roosters strike it up, playing furiously with Jack on the mandolin, Kieran on the fiddle, and Rob and Chester leap on the stage to dance.

And they are really soaring when the lights go out.

The band keeps playing and Tommy goes on singing but it falls apart there in the dark and then nobody plays or sings anything. In the silence, they hear Nepo's paws click across the stage. Jack starts playing mandolin again and Tommy starts singing again and everybody laughs again.

The bartender finds his way into the back room with a flashlight, opens the fuse box, and starts flicking switches. Nothing happens. The bartender hears footsteps in the dark and swivels the beam around onto Eric.

"I have loads of candles at the lodge," he says. The flashlight beam moves over a bit and Ellen is there too.

"Do ya?" The bartender holds the flashlight under his chin so they can see him.

"We'll be right back." Eric and Ellen hold hands and weave their way through the pub, squeezing between people bumping into each other under the green glow of the emergency exit lights, and then they are out in the rain and wind again, which has only gotten stronger and wilder.

Eric puts an arm around Ellen and moves her in the direction of the Rose Lodge. He knows where he's going, having made this trip late at night, drunk, from a graveyard.

The Rose Lodge sign is just ahead, blurry and unlit in the rain.

CANDLES

IN MARY'S OFFICE, everyone has their feet up on her candlelit desk and the whiskey has made the circle of guests a few times. Mary has changed into her thick red robe and her bare toes are twinkling warm up near the candles.

"I hope the lights stay off," she says. "I like it like this. The lights go out and everyone lets their hair down!"

They hear the front door crash open and shut and then Eric and Ellen are in the candlelight with them, wet and out of breath. Eric introduces Ellen to the guests and sits down with Mary.

"You know the music we've been hearing? We were just there. It's around the corner on Western Road. They were in the middle of a song when they lost their power and they didn't give a shit either, sorry, but they laughed and the band went on playing and singing. How many candles do we have? I told the barman I'd bring him some. The pub's all in the dark."

"We have six boxes of candles, Eric. And we'll take the van so you and Ellen can dry out." Mary stands up and smiles at her table of guests.

"And you are all invited to a *new* party! Would you be so kind as to help us carry some boxes of candles out to the van?"

The front door opens again and they hear footsteps coming slowly towards the office. A man with a hat pulled low and dripping shows up in the office door holding a box.

"Need some candles, Mary? You know how it is—the light you take is equal to the candles you ... well ... *you* know what I mean." The man puts the box on the desk, takes off his hat, and puts a hand on Eric's shoulder.

"How's the new job then, son? Mary says you're doin' fine. And I am sure that you'll rise and shine!" Eric laughs and introduces the man to Ellen.

And then Mary drives Phillip, Eric and Ellen, the guests, and seven boxes of candles around the corner to the pub, still in her robe with her bare foot on the gas.

CORK

NO ONE HAS LEFT Shane's Pub.

They are all walking around bumping into each other in the strange green light overhead and getting to know each other. Jack is still on the stage picking at his mandolin and the piano player softly joins him. The sax player has passed out in a chair and the other Roosters are mixing with the crowd. Kieran and Julie and Tommy and Sondra are lying on the stage talking. Declan and Donal are at a corner table with the v-neck sweater sisters. Rob and Chester drink by the window and watch the rain outside. They clink glasses.

A van drives up to the front door.

Mary gets out, opens the back of the van, and takes out a box, followed by Phillip. Then Eric and Ellen do the same, carrying boxes into the pub, followed by the guests of the lodge, some of them in pajamas and robes.

Jack and the piano player stop playing as they watch them come in, walk into the middle of the room and start opening the boxes. The room is quiet as everyone watches these people open the boxes and take out candles. They all watch Mary light a candle and pass it to someone near and then the others light candles and pass those candles around and the room starts to be less green and more candlelit. No one says anything, but people are coming and helping open the boxes and matches are struck and lighters are lit and the candles are floating all around the room in all directions, towards every dark corner. And still, no one is talking. They hear the rain on the roof and they hear each other's footsteps and chairs scrape back out of the way as they set the candles up all over the pub, on the bar, on the stage, on each table. The Roosters are each carrying a candle through the room as are Declan and Donal and Julie and Kieran and Sondra and Tommy and now Chester and Rob come over to the boxes and take candles. Eric lights candles for Chester and Rob who, for some reason, bow to each other before they move off in different directions with their candles, looking for somewhere to place them. The candles are all lit now, every corner of the room glowing and flickering.

And still, no one is talking.

Everyone in the pub stands still listening to the rain and looking around at the candles everywhere, their flickering the only movement in the room. They look at the candles and the light they've made all around the room and then they look at each other a bit, but not too directly, leaving each other alone, staying each of them apart, but together in the room. Sondra looks across the room at Nepo, who sits far away by himself, quietly gazing and blinking at the candles. Kieran and Julie are standing next to each other with their eyes closed. Declan and Donal are standing together too, arms around each other. Tommy is on stage holding a candle in both hands and looking out over the room. Mary and Eric and Ellen and the Rose Lodge guests sit in a circle by the empty candle boxes and stare into their candles on the floor. Jack sits up on the stage with Tommy, also staring at his candle. Rob sits at a table by himself holding a candle and shaking his head, smiling, and crying, then he starts laughing.

And now everyone laughs, flickering some of the candles. Then it's quiet again, and they listen to the rain.

Tommy says something to the piano player, then walks down to the middle of the pub and into the middle of the empty candle boxes. The piano player gently starts to play, and the guitar player comes along soft. Tommy goes to Mary and kisses the top of her head. "Thanks for the light Mary, right everybody?" They all thank her as well. Now Kieran is inside the music with his fiddle, and other instruments are blending in. Tommy sits on the edge of a table with his head down and waits as the band plays a long building introduction to "My Lagan Love."

Tommy sings the song very slowly with his eyes closed, his face floating in the candlelight.

When the song ends, Tommy lies down on the floor where he's been singing and Sondra comes to him and lies down with him. Mary sits in a chair by them, smiling and smiling and smiling as Eric and Ellen lie nearby in each other's arms. Some people pass out in chairs, the Roosters go to sleep on the stage, the sax player still with his sunglasses on. Declan and Donal sit with Jack, who is wide awake and ready for talk, and the brothers quietly ask him all about Cork. Rob and Nepo curl up and begin snoring together. Kieran and Julie, the waitresses, and a few others stand at the bar talking, and the bartender pours free drinks this morning.

It's very still in the low light of the pub and the flames on the candles are tall.

THE END, THE BEGINNING

LATER, CHESTER STANDS in his blue corduroy robe looking out through the rough window of his stone house and he sees all of the city below. The sun's up and he'll be in bed soon. First, though, he lights up the cigar from Kirby's Pub in Tralee. A celebration cigar. Chester is fifty today.

He moved here to end everything normal in his life.

"... too late to stop now."

Into the Mystic
Van Morrison

Chris Coulson lives in Santa Fe, New Mexico, where it's proven that getting older is nothing to worry about. Something he's known all along, in that he felt old way too young, but that *joy* would carry him through, and now that he's older, because of joy, he feels younger. Something like that.
Something Coulson experienced in Ireland, too.